Dan L. Walker

ALASKA
NORTHWEST
BOOKS®

Library of Congress Cataloging-in-Publication Data

Names: Walker, Dan, 1947- author.
Title: Secondhand summer / by Dan L Walker.
Description: Portland, Oregon : Alaska Northwest Books, [2016] | Summary: Sam, a twelve-year-old boy who loved the homestead fishing life he left behind when his father died, moves to the big city of Anchorage where new friends lead him on forays into crime, and leave him feeling wilder and wiser.
Identifiers: LCCN 2015049230 (print) | LCCN 2016014940 (ebook) | ISBN 9781943328420 (pbk.) | ISBN 9781943328437 (e-book) | ISBN 9781943328796 (hardbound)
Subjects: | CYAC: Coming of age--Fiction. | Grief--Fiction. | Alaska--Fiction.
Classification: LCC PZ7.1.W348 Se 2016 (print) | LCC PZ7.1.W348 (ebook) | DDC
    [Fic]--dc23
LC record available at http://lccn.loc.gov/2015049230

Edited by Michelle McCann
Designed by Vicki Knapton
Cover illustrations by Karen DeWitz

Published by Alaska Northwest Books®
An imprint of

GRAPHIC ARTS
BOOKS®

P.O. Box 56118
Portland, Oregon 97238-6118
503-254-5591
www.graphicartsbooks.com

To my father, Chet Walker, whose legend
guided me long after he left this earth.

Acknowledgments

This book is a product of many people who invested in the writer and his work. *Secondhand Summer* was fueled by the tireless support of Madelyn, my wife, and carried forward by the forever-patient editor, Michelle McCann. Mary Armstrong and Nancy Fisher gave me the reader's perspective, and Kathy Tillman Corp provided unwavering inspiration, insight, and encouragement. Twenty-two years spent with adolescent students reminded me daily what those middle school years were like. Of course, I nod to my mother who always knew I had it in me.

Chapter 1

The last day I saw my father alive he was in a wooden dory coming through the swells to the beach. Sometimes the loaded dory dropped out of sight as it pushed through the waves, so my father appeared to walk across the water toward us. Over the nets stacked in the bow, I could see his hat pushed back to show his smile. There would be few fish in the boat, maybe a dozen late run cohos, the last lean pickings of a used up season. The rest of the load was nets, buoys, and anchors coming in for the last time that year.

Joe and I waited on the beach, thinking it was just the end of a fishing season. We had no way of knowing that it was the end of everything we knew.

Joe sat in the jeep with his arms hung on the wheel, just like he was finishing his time on the beach, his time at home. He was eighteen and restless to move on.

"I wish he'd let me go out," I said. "For the last run anyway."

"You'll get your chance next year, Humpy. Then you'll be sorry. You'll have your fill real fast."

"Nah, it'll probably be just you and Dad again with me on the beach picking the low tide sets. Even on the nice days Mom will say no." She had been raised on the beach sites and watched two brothers drown when a dory flipped in the surf and trapped them beneath it.

"Don't count on it."

"Whaddaya mean?"

"What the hell do you think I mean?" Joe leaned out of the jeep at me. "I'm hittin' the road."

"Anchorage?" Some road, I thought.

"Damn straight."

The sun and tide were falling and an evening breeze had kicked up some chop around the one red keg buoy still anchored between the boat and the beach. The boat hovered while Dad lifted the buoy clear of the water and hauled the line in hand over hand. His shoulders and stance were broad as he braced against the roll of the swells and the rocking boat. He was full of power when the sea flexed beneath him, and the buoy line was a bridle on it. He hefted the sandbag into the dory with a spray of water and gray bottom mud, then turned toward us with a wave of his hand. I winced to see him lifting that way.

"Keep your mouth shut, ya hear," Joe said. He fired up the jeep and jerked it into gear. "This is between me and Him."

Joe always called Dad "Him." As if he wasn't really our father, pushing him away as part of his escape.

I try to imagine how Joe remembers him now, but I can't. I just see him the way I remember him, coming in through the chop in his rain pants and the wool sweater cut off at the elbows. He was too far away for the weakness to show in his face. One hand gripped the tiller while the other, brown and cracked like old cedar, waved to us in the sunset. Joe was like him but taller and leaner, the next best thing.

We unloaded the nets when Dad came in. Then we dragged the boat up high on the beach with the jeep. Joe and I were trying to do most of the lifting like Mom had told us. Last October, Dad had a heart attack, and he'd spent the winter recovering. Mom and the doctor told him not to fish, but he wasn't that kind.

I emptied out the odds and ends of tools and bailing buckets that spent the summer in the boat. Joe and Dad unbolted the outboard motor and toted it and the gas cans into the plywood shed that squatted back in the alders along the bluff. With the help of the jeep, the three of us flipped the boat over on its gunwales so it rested on a pair of driftwood logs. Then Dad padlocked the shed and it was done. The last eight fish of the summer lay in the back of the jeep for canning, and when Dad passed me and tousled my head, I savored the last sweet smell of man sweat, salt, and salmon. The season was over.

Dad jumped into the jeep and honked the horn. "I'll take the bluff," I said. The jeep had to take the road up the creek bed through the bluff to the highway, but a person on foot could walk a hundred yards up the beach and climb a steep trail to our backyard. From where I stood on the beach the galvanized metal roof of our house was just visible through a wedge of spruce trees.

"Suit yourself, Humpy!" Dad yelled above the roar of the motor. Joe nodded his head approvingly. Maybe he was going to give Dad the word on the way home and didn't want an audience. I hoped not. It would be good if we had the last night of the season without a fight, and it would be a fight. Or so I thought.

Our one-story log house squatted in the fireweed and wild geraniums on the bluff overlooking the inlet. From the back porch, we could look down on the fishermen, their open dories like water-birds all pointy in the front and wide behind, the cork lines of their nets like strings of beads across the tide. Farther out, the drift boats fished the tide rips that ran like rivers of current and had names like "clear muddy" and "middle rip." Beyond them the giant container ships steamed up and down Cook Inlet to and from Anchorage. On the horizon stood two giant volcanoes with their noses pushed up in the clouds, spouting occasional puffs of steam. In the long light of a clear summer evening, the bluff seemed on the rim of the world and the boats and mountains fell away before me.

In the summer, we practically lived on the beach where the salmon ran in great schools along the shore, and we stretched nets from the beach to catch them. Each day I made a dozen trips up and down the bluff trail fetching tools, hauling food and messages. The base of the trail was a scramble of loose sand and coal chunks fallen from the bluff above. Where the trail ran over sandstone, there were steps chopped in it and a rope for safety; I'd quit using the rope last summer after weeks of Joe's teasing. From there, I could scramble on all fours up a washout and over the lip to our backyard.

To the right was the garden where Mom spent most of her summer with her back to the water. To the left was the house guarded by giant spruces and surrounded with beds of pansies, poppies, irises, and forget-me-nots.

Usually when I climbed the bluff, I was escaping pirates or Nazi soldiers, but that day I was all in the present and laden with the empty end of summer. I paused and hung on the rope, gazing down the inlet. The Fergusons were still out hauling buoys and the Leman's 4X4 was dragging a dory out of the breakers toward the bluff. In a week, the beaches would be empty, and the only tracks on the beach would be those of the jeeps collecting coal for the winter. And that wasn't nearly as much fun as fishing.

I was watching the water, contemplating this passing of summer when Dad had his second heart attack. If I had ridden in the jeep I would have been there but instead I was on the bluff looking at the water, so I missed seeing my dad one last time. He and Joe had made it to the gravel shoulder of the highway before he stopped the jeep, grabbed his chest, and collapsed. I guess that's why I remember it all so well. I remember how he looked coming in through swells with his hat tipped back and his brown hand waving. Waving to me, waving good-bye.

By the time I clambered up to the house, the station wagon was tearing out of the driveway with Joe at the wheel, leaving my older sister, Mary, standing on the porch screaming after it, "Daddy, Daddy, Daddy!" Suddenly, I couldn't breathe.

✴ ✴

Dad's first heart attack had come ten months before. He hadn't come home from the hospital until Thanksgiving, but when he did we thought our troubles were over. As the evenings grew longer and the sun wasn't much brighter than the moon, my father lost his warmth. He was weak and pale and angry, as if the winter had entered his soul and chilled his spirit. Our family was soon trapped in the midst of night and cold. The happy card games were gone; talk and laughter were muted. That entire winter, it seemed, we sat at my father's side and waited.

Then, only weeks before summer when the days grew warm and light, we saw signs of hope. Dad seemed to face down the demons in his body and his familiar strength returned. His, and therefore our, infallibility remained untarnished. We would fish on. We did fish that summer, and I spent most of the summer on the beach.

It was the last day of salmon season when death passed among us. One week later, we buried him behind the church in a grave that overlooked Cook Inlet.

Chapter 2

Mom broke the news one Sunday in March when we were sitting at the kitchen table eating apple Betty for dessert. Joe was there, Mary, Mom, and me. Only Dad was missing, and we hadn't gotten used to that yet.

"We have to move to Anchorage," said Mom. Her voice was soft but strong, and I can't think of a much harder thing she ever had to say. "You kids can stay with the Browns until school is over. But I'm going to have to go get a job. You know there is nothing here, no work for a woman, nothing that pays anything." The strength was gone suddenly from her voice. She looked around the cabin with tears filling her eyes and leaking down her cheeks. "You'll never know how hard this is for me. To lose him like this, and then this too. Your father loved it here, you know."

I could only think of how it felt to hug her, how she was soft on the outside and hard underneath. Dad's hugs were just hard, no softness, their strength right out front. I thought she could use a hug just then, but one from me wouldn't help much.

Joe leaned back on his chair and looked at the ceiling. "It makes sense to me," he said. Of course, it was fine with him. He had stayed too long already. "It'll be better, you'll see."

I saw Mom's pain as she swept the hair back from her face and held the coffee cup to her lips so that the steam from it rose into her nose and eyes. She did that when she was choosing careful words. "We don't all feel that way, Joe. We don't all *want* to leave."

"He'll be here forever," I heard myself say, "and we'll be back."

I don't know why I said it that way, like a kid could make decisions about such things, about anything, but Dad was buried on the bluff above the inlet. The log house he built and the land he cleared, the smokehouse and all of it would be here. It wasn't going away.

Mary erupted instead of speaking, as she always seemed to do. "Joe doesn't care about anyone but himself, Mom. You know that. No one cares what I want. No one asks me!"

"Now Mary."

"Daddy wouldn't want us to leave," said Mary. She turned a hard stare at the three of us at the table. "He built this place for us, and this is where we should stay."

I thought Mom was going to cry again. "I want to stay too, Mary, but your father would expect us to do what we had to do to get by. He didn't like going doodle-bugging for an oil company, off in the middle of nowhere all winter either. But he did it to support this family. And we are going to do what we have to."

Joe was suddenly restless and he rose to tend the fire. He opened the stove, exposing the red coals and jabbed them with a poker, creating a shower of sparks. Then he slammed the stove door with a bang, pulled on Dad's wool coat, and passed through the snow porch to the cold and silence of the winter night.

It was done. The talk at the kitchen table was just talk. As sure as the sunrise, we were moving to Anchorage. The wind in the trees was stronger now, and I could hear the snow brushing against the windows, and I wondered if it would be winter forever.

It was the darkest of winters, this winter after Dad died. The nights were endless and the sun of the day had no warmth. Only the wind seemed to move, moaning as it swept across the muskegs searching for spring.

During the long evenings I hid from the cold of death and winter by reading tales of the mountain men, and I studied their lives in our battered *Compton's Encyclopedia*. I walked in the tracks of Lewis and Clark, and slept in the camp of John Colter. I laid trap for beaver with Joe Meek, greatest of the frontiersmen.

I decided I could be a mountain man, so I ventured beyond the shoveled paths and into the sleeping timber. The chickadees were the only sign of life as I crossed over places where I had played in the summer, and I walked taller as I passed deeper into the forest. I used to be scared of the shadowed maze of trees but now the birches and alders were stripped naked, and I could see deep into the woods, much farther than during the summer.

Small trails ran around the trees and under the brush. And I knew the broad tracks and black scat pellets of rabbit. A shadow moved and then froze. A rabbit saw me. I froze too and our eyes locked for a moment. I made a plan.

In the shed I found snares hanging in a corner, tinted with rust and long forgotten. I remembered pictures from books showing how they should be hung, and I tried to recall each detail as I separated the long pieces of wire with their tiny lassoes at the end. There were six in all, and I stretched each full length on the rough workbench beside the coffee cans full of nails and bolts and strange magical parts that only a father could put to use and therefore have reason to save. The shed had been Dad's quiet place, and I felt a touch of guilt for the times I interrupted that silence, "What's that do? Why is metal heavy? Will I ever be big as you?" He would nod and answer or nod and not answer without looking up from his work.

I had questions now, but they went unasked as I oiled the snares like Dad would have. I could smell his Prince Albert cigarettes and hear the curses he used on the rusty bolts and broken engine parts. I could feel his presence among his tools.

I set my snares by hanging them from bushes along the narrow little paths that ran under the moose brush and devil's club where larger animals wouldn't go. Some I tied on bushes bent over springlike and anchored with a notched stick. Others hung loose from the branches above. Sometimes, I used sticks to build a tiny fence along the trail through the snow. When a rabbit ran along the trail he was supposed to run his head into the noose until it tightened around his neck and choked him.

Each day, I went directly from the school bus to check my traplines. The dusk came early in the clearing and darkness had settled among the trees, making the giant spruces seem taller. I imagined sinister creatures hiding beneath them. On especially dark evenings I ran the whole trail in ten minutes, not stopping, just slowing down for a quick glance as I passed each snare. I was ashamed of the fear that sometimes grabbed me. I liked the snares and the trail and the time alone; I just didn't like the woods in the dark.

The great adventure stories and my daydreams about them never showed that fear. I had to wonder, were the mountain men ever afraid of what could be out in the night beyond the light of their tiny campfire? Did they ever cower under blankets, wishing they were home in bed with people around them? The woods did that to me. Every shadowed tree, each gust of wind, every frightened thrush made me jump and tremble.

On one early spring evening, the winds off the inlet had filled most of the trails with snow, and I had to pick my way carefully, following the flags of plastic ribbon that marked the path through the forest. By now the days were longer, but there was little warmth from the sun, and the air bit at my cheeks.

I'd been trapping for weeks and had caught nothing, so I was complacent, expecting nothing, only half paying attention to the snares as I passed them. Then there it was!

The rabbit was dead. He lay stiff, frozen in an unfinished lunge with my snare cinched around his neck, strangling the last of his breath. It was just a meal now, rabbit stew lying cold on the snow. I stepped back, a lump of nausea rising in my throat. My first prey was dead before me, and I couldn't touch it. I had found the run and set the snare, but I couldn't touch the catch. I didn't want to handle the rabbit I had killed, but I had to. I had to be a hunter, to take possession. I leaned forward and cautiously lifted one leg. The fur was soft like a cat's, but beneath was solid like someone had stuffed a wooden cutout of a rabbit in a real rabbit's fur. The eyes were real though, and the tiny crystal of blood frozen to the lips was real.

I forgot how cold it was. The nausea was passing, and I forgot that I had lost my father. I forgot everything but the dead rabbit, and I wanted to make a fire and eat it right there.

Gingerly I took the wire in two fingers and lifted the head. The snare wire was buried in the white fur and traces of blood tinted it pink. I gagged a little as I loosened the noose and pulled the carcass free. The animal was heavy and long, so I had to hold my arm up as I shuffled toward the house, changing hands every few steps.

I climbed over the berm pile and stopped to rest my arm. Dead things were heavy. I squatted in a small depression in the pile of stumps and brush that formed a low wall around our clearing. In the summer a large elderberry shaded this place and the fireweed and raspberries made it private. Wild grass formed a soft bed for daydreaming. It was there that I had dreamed of crossing the Rockies to trap for beaver, making detailed lists of gunpowder, salt pork, and trade beads. Gazing at the sky I could enumerate each detail of my outfit and weapons. I fought Indians and Hudson's Bay Company trappers. But that was the summer; this day was real, and I passed over that dreaming place.

It was a short walk across the clearing to the house. I could see the tiny hump of it squatting in the snow, a rectangular log box with a pitched roof. Out behind was the outhouse and beyond that a dory turned over and hidden in the snow beside the smokehouse.

The light in the kitchen window made a pale square of gold in the snow, and my mother's shadow passed through it. She waved when she saw me. I held up the rabbit and saw her smile.

"Don't you bring that thing in here," she said, catching me at the door. She smelled of homemade food and warmth, and the heat of the kitchen washed around her like surf. "My that's a big one," she added. "I guess I know what I'm cooking tomorrow night."

The darkness around her eyes reminded me of our loss, and I was filled with a sense of panic. There was no father at this house to help me clean the rabbit. Dad would have known how to butcher the animal and probably would have told me a story while he did it.

"You remember how to clean them, right?"

"Yeah, no problem," I lied.

I turned back to the forest, and beneath a giant spruce I used my knife to open the rabbit and expose the innards. They were cold, nearly frozen, and I had to tug and tear to pull the strange slimy shapes out of the cavity formed by the creature's ribs. I was making a mess of it, ripping meat and hide, splattering myself with blood. I knew the skin should come off in one smooth slip like taking off one-piece long johns, but I didn't know how, and there was no Dad there in that cold winter evening to show me.

I looked across the snow to the back edge of the clearing where the berm pile made a shadow in the pale light of evening. I didn't feel anything like a mountain man. My feet were cold and it was dark under the trees where the night started early. There were cold tears on my cheeks. I knew that Dad would insist that the guts be left back in the trees away from the cabin where scavengers could get them. He would have turned grouchy if I complained.

Several yards into the shadowed forest I threw the rabbit guts across the snow where they spread a shameful stain. I walked slowly back to the house with my rabbit in my hand and wondered how many days I had left. I knew we couldn't stay. Soon I would have to put away my snares and say good-bye to the cabin in the woods that I was just beginning to come to know.

As if reading my mind, Mom confirmed my fears when I returned to the house. She took the rabbit and laid it in a pan of cold water. As she washed her hands she leaned against the sink and smiled the first real smile I'd seen in several weeks. "Are you proud of yourself, bringing home dinner like a man?"

"I hope I gutted it okay," I said.

"It's just fine." She moved across the room shortening the distance between us. "Sam, you'll have to pull your snares in a few days."

I nodded my answer, feeling the comfort of her presence and the warmth of the fire in the woodstove. I knew she was heading to Anchorage to start a job, and we kids were to be farmed out with friends until we finished the school year.

Perhaps it was the purity of a sleeping forest in winter, or maybe it was just the safe, warm feeling of the cabin itself with its memory of Dad's laugh and the taste of his cream and sugar coffee. For whatever reason, the homestead was a good place to be, especially for a guy like me. Then I knew that in this, my first time in the woods alone, long before the end of winter's shadow, I had started a new part of my life.

Chapter 3

A t the end of March, Joe left home for Anchorage. It was a quiet, casual departure as if he was just going to the beach site for a couple of days instead of moving out on his own to the city two hundred miles away. Mom, Mary, and I were still on the porch and the sound of his car had just faded when Art Mitkof pulled up in his green Chevy pickup. He came in and sat at the table as he often did on winter mornings, sipping his sweetened coffee while Mom worked.

Mom started washing dishes, then worked restlessly across the kitchen to tend pans of rising bread. She had taken to baking bread again, the one thing she truly loved to do. There was even a touch of color back in her cheeks.

Art rubbed his pant leg with a nervous hand. "Spring's out there somewhere," he said. "Soon be time to hang some new web."

"John always said winter was for hanging web," said Mom. "Spring seems kinda late."

Art had grown up in Ninilchik. He was part Russian and

part Dena'ina Indian, with his slick black hair and thin mustache. He had fished the beach beside us all my life. "Yeah, John, he was always a little ahead o' me on that one."

"That was his way." Mom leaned on her bread dough and took a deep breath.

Art ran a handful of fingers through his hair and rubbed the back of his neck. "I gotta tell ya," he said, "I don't like to see you sell off like this."

Mom slammed a fist into the bread dough and turned to face him. "Art, I gotta sell the fish sites and go to Anchorage. There's no two ways about it. What am I going to live on here? I can't fish. I'm not about to put myself in a dory and pretend I know what I'm doing. It's not what I want, Art. I just don't see another way. We are keeping the land and the house, but the fish sites gotta go."

Her chubby body seemed to sag in the dress she wore. "Joe's already gone to Anchorage to get a construction job. Without him, fishing's out of the question. You know I can't run that skiff, much less set a net. Sam here is eager, but he doesn't have the beef for it, and I sure can't afford to hire a hand. Those sites barely fed us as it was, and John still had to hire on to that oil exploration crew and go doodle-buggin' most every winter."

"You know I'd help you," said Art. I could see his face as he imagined himself trying to keep his nets mended and in the water while he babysat the Barger clan.

"Art, you're a doll, but face it, you can't hardly get around to your own work much less help me."

I could see Mom had hurt his feelings, but she was right. Dad always said the only thing Art would work at was fishing and sometimes even that got to be too much like work. I saw him look away out the window and down the road like he hoped Dad would pull into the driveway.

"I can take Joe's place in the skiff," I said. I took a seat at the table as if invited. "I could. I know how to run the motor; I can set the nets, me and Mary." Just saying it put a knot in my stomach, and I knew I was wasting my breath.

There would be new faces in the rain gear at the beach this summer. Someone else would haul our gillnets off the racks and into the boats. Someone else would run the boats that pulled the nets out from shore. Someone else would have my bunk in the shack on the beach, where they'd sleep every chance they got, so they could wake at every change of the tide to pick fish from the nets, pull the nets out of the water, set the nets back in the water. Someone else would learn that days didn't matter, and by July they'd only know tides and the opening and closing of the fishing period.

Someone else would have that odor of salmon fishing; the sweet ocean cologne of sand, salt, and fish. The smell filled your pores until even a good hot bath wouldn't drive it out, and people could tell that you were a fisherman. Someone else would have that odor this summer. I wouldn't be there when the tide was running, and the nets were bent into a bow. I wouldn't be mending the web, patching holes that let fish escape, costing money. Dad would say, "No time to sleep when the net's in rags. Can't make money with a ragged net."

I would just be a regular kid at a time I was ready to be more than a regular kid, to be a fisherman. I wanted to be in the bow of the dory when the surf was running and the waves were higher than Dad's head. That's the sea my mother feared. She believed she'd die in that water, and she was scared for me too.

"You kids stay out of the boats," she insisted every spring when she took us to the beach cabin for the first time. "You fall in that water and you'll freeze to death in a minute."

She passed her fears on to me with her lectures, and I avoided the water until the urge to be older and bolder grew too strong. It was as if her phobia finally pushed me toward the sea. The first calm day of 1964, I talked my way over the gunwale and into the open dory as it bobbed in the surf. I lay in the belly of a great sea creature with ribs of spruce and a skin of plywood. The aroma of fish was like a drug that reeked of adventure.

Mom came stomping down the beach from the cabin, yelling at Dad. "John Barger," she growled, "you know how I feel about those kids being out on the water."

Dad was leaning on the gunwale, rocking with it up and down on the edge of the water. "I know," he said. "I also know that you're wrong. How are we supposed to be fishermen and sit on the beach?" I hung over the bow and looked into the sand as they fought. When the water was shallow the land beneath it was bright and visible, then surges of murky water came in, and I saw nothing.

"What if that boat tips? What if the motor stops, or you spring a leak? What are you going to tell me then? 'I'm sorry, Arlene, but your kids drowned because we have to go fishing'."

Dad stomped off, muttering, "Don't know why in the hell she even let 'em out of diapers. Wants 'em to be babies forever."

I went out anyway, splashing through the meager waves of a sunny day, tasting salt water when it fell on our faces like rain, pretending I was helping when actually I just got in the way, pretending I was strong and able when I was weak and scared. Mom went home and tended her garden rather than pace the beach and watch her youngest baby porpoising around with the men who belonged out where the danger was.

We approached the end of each net and lifted it onboard, first the cork line and then the rest of the web and the lead line, and hopefully some fish. We pulled the boat along the net so it passed over one gunwale and then the other and back in the water to fish another tide. Some salmon were tangled and dead with the web choking them into grotesque shapes. That made me glad to see the live ones held only by a single mesh at their gills, flashing silver torpedoes turning more green-like on the bottom of the skiff. They piled up around our feet, sliding back and forth with the rock of the boat.

"Striker there!" yelled Joe from the stern and we looked up from the net to see a flashing tail thrash at the cork line as a fresh salmon slammed into the wall of the net. I cheered.

Another fish jumped south of the net, and I wondered as it leaped again, driving toward our net, and it rammed in splashing and thrashing. "Striker!" I cried, but the fish was small and squirted through to jump again north of the net.

"Just a stupid humpy," sneered Joe.

"How do you know?"

"Humpies almost always squirt through. They're like you, too small to be worth anything."

"All fish are money fish, Joe," Dad said, "even little pinks. Just like Sam here. He's kind of a humpy." He tousled my hair and laughed. He called me "Humpy" all summer. Then everybody did.

Humpy Barger, a good name for a salmon fisherman, I figured. No one else in the family had a nickname; I treasured it as my father's gift. I would be like I remembered him, standing spraddle-legged in the boat with sleeves cut off at the elbows and the patched rain pants hanging down over rubber boots. A scruffy beard, the battered dory, and the magic smell of the salmon summer I wouldn't have because my boat was empty.

Leaving the beach was the first step in letting myself leave this place on Cook Inlet, these people in their log cabins and trailer houses, these woods full of mystery. The town I was leaving wasn't really a town at all. A person driving through Ninilchik would see a gas station, a café, and a couple of churches. The houses were strung out along the highway or hidden on bad back roads too muddy to drive much of the time in the spring.

There were people there too, people with names and lives mixed with mine, kids I'd been babies with, like we were hairs on the same head. I knew people's trucks and jeeps and carryalls; I knew their skiffs and winter coats, which men smoked Camels or rolled their own Prince Albert, who made the best sticky buns and the worst pie. All these important things wouldn't matter any more. Even Becky.

Becky was the only girl in my class that looked like she might be a woman someday. All the others were gawky little girls with silly faces and skinny legs. But Becky filled out her jeans, and her sweaters didn't lie flat on her chest. Right after Christmas I got to sit by her during a movie about Holland.

"I wish I had a coat like that," I said, pointing to a boy in a blue short jacket like the kid on the paint cans.

"You'd be so cute," she teased.

We giggled and she touched my arm. With this kind of encouragement I began to perform. I named each strange character after someone in town. It was the best of my eighth grade antics, and sitting with Becky in the near dark was close to total perfection. After that day she sat by me during school movies and gave me secret glances in class. She let me give her a piece of ivory that I found on the beach, and she wore it around her neck on a chain.

When Dad died and I came back to school with that everybody's-looking-at-me feeling, she acted normal as ever. She and Harry Munson were the ones who just treated me the same as ever. Harry was either my best friend or worst enemy depending on the day, or even the time of day.

Harry was born and raised in Ninilchik but had some magic that made it seem that he was from somewhere else, somewhere far away enough to be unreal, somewhere like Seattle or California. He was tall and athletic with natural waves to his hair, and he kept it combed like a high schooler. His clothes were from the catalog, not homemade or hand-me-downs, and he wore loafers.

Harry and I invented the game "Run the Gauntlet," which made us leaders in the school, and we tended to swagger. Run the Gauntlet was a reenactment of the challenge used by the Iroquois and Huron Indians in my late night readings. The captured warrior was given a chance of freedom by running between lines of angry people armed with fists, clubs, and feet. The warrior had only to reach the end of the brutal lines and run to freedom. It seemed the perfect game for us middle schoolers.

We were playing our daily version of the game and I was the captured warrior. I dashed at the narrow opening in the line, knocking down two seventh graders right at the start. Bart and Jimmy scored good hits on my back. I was twisting and dodging my way to daylight when Harry stretched out a long leg and tripped me. I went down hard in the packed snow. The laughter and jeers were part of the game. When Harry leaned down to help me up, I saw Becky laughing with the others.

"By the way," Harry said, "did I tell you Becky was at church last night? We held hands all through Pastor Peterson's slide show about his trip to Jerusalem."

The truth of it didn't matter to me, or him. Saying it, imagining it, was enough. I came up swinging and caught Harry by surprise with a fist in the stomach. He nearly fell and I pranced in front of him with my fists raised. "Come on, you liar!" I snarled. He stuck out his chin and charged.

"Liar? Nobody calls me that."

Any friendship between us melted into rage. We pushed and thumped and slugged until we were both dirty and out of breath. Finally I threw one lucky punch that caught my best friend in the nose and drew blood. Our classmates were whooping and yelling then were silent. Only then did I realize that the other kids were running for school and the principal was running for us.

"I know losing a father is tough on a boy," said Mr. Morris, the fat principal, staring at me over his eyeglasses from behind his metal desk, "but you've got to learn to sit on that anger and let things pass. I know these are rough times, with your dad gone and all, but look at you, brawling with one of your pals like this."

I looked at him confused and irritated, and my jutting lower lip probably showed it. What did my fight with Harry have to do with Dad?

He turned to Harry. "Mr. Munson, I'd appreciate it if you would show some consideration for a grieving friend. You have got to understand that Sam needs us, each and every one of the people in his life, to help him through this. He has enough challenges right now."

Neither of us was sure what he was talking about, but it was obvious that we weren't getting in trouble. Mr. Morris shook his head in surrender and waved a tired hand.

"Go on now, get back to class, and let's have no more of this."

That afternoon we had another movie in class: *Barges in the Rhine.*

"Did you get in trouble?" Becky whispered, leaning close so I could feel her hair brush my arm.

"No, but no thanks to you."

"Me? What did I do?" We both jerked around when Mr. Scott paused mid-sentence and everyone stared right at us.

The dreary monologue about hauling coal and wheat through Europe continued. "Harry told me," I hissed.

"Told you what?"

"About last night. You sitting with him at church."

"So!"

I waited a full three slide frames before I delivered the crushing blow. "That's why I hit him."

Fighting with Harry got me through that last couple of months. Hardly a day went by that we didn't have some kind of shoving match, and sometimes they turned to full-blown fist-fights. Of course, he said he won most of the fights, but Becky didn't give back the piece of ivory, and she didn't sit by him during any of the movies.

Mr. Morris did a lot of coddling, patting me on the back and letting me off easy when I acted up in class. One time he held me in class during recess. He sat on the edge of the desk and fiddled with the crease in his pants. "You know, Sam, I lost my dad too when I was very young. I know what you're going through."

"Yeah. At least he won't have to go to your funeral."

"Huh? I don't understand."

"My grandpa did. He had to go to his son's funeral. Just seems kinda weird, that's all."

I know he didn't understand. I probably made no sense at all. Mr. Morris just shook his head and nodded. He didn't speak to me again until the last day of school then he called me aside. "Samuel, I have a gift for you," he said, handing me a book from one of those church publishers. I think he was glad to see the last of me when the final school bell rang and we all ran screaming into the sunlight of summer vacation.

I never read the book, but I kept a card that Becky gave me. It was a valentine with a red heart and a Cupid with wings. She signed it, "Your girlfriend, Becky."

Chapter 4

On the last day of May, the Bargers drove down Hollywood Drive to our new home in the Hollywood Arms Apartments. Unfortunately, Hollywood Drive in Anchorage, Alaska, had no resemblance to the Hollywood that the rest of the world knew about. Ours was one of dozens of two-story apartment buildings scattered like Monopoly hotels on Government Hill across Ship Creek from downtown Anchorage.

We drove into Anchorage from the south and except for the mountains behind it, Anchorage looked like a city in a geography book, with neighborhoods and groceries stores and gas stations. As we neared downtown, the buildings closed in around our car, and on every block it seemed a building had collapsed or stood empty, damaged by the big earthquake the year before. Suddenly, the downtown ended, and the stores and other building were gone. Most of them were crumbled by the quake and then hauled away in dump trucks. It left a bare hill right on the edge of busy downtown.

The hill leading down to the railroad and the docks was

empty. At the base of this hill, Ship Creek crossed under the railroad tracks, past the docks and the rail yards, and slid through the mudflats into Cook Inlet. We drove across and up the opposite bluff to Government Hill, where most of the traffic was headed for the air force base. Our neighborhood was on the bluff above the railroad yard and two blocks from Elmendorf Air Force Base. Hollywood Drive seemed, even to a bush kid, to be in the middle of nowhere going nowhere.

We parked in front of the Hollywood Arms and started unloading the car. Mary complained as soon as Mom was out of earshot. "You notice nobody asked what *we* wanted? This place is a dump. I can just imagine what the kids are like."

"It's not so bad," I said.

"Not so bad! When you get to be my age, Humpy, you'll be more particular. Peeling paint the color of chicken vomit, dirty, broken windows? It's a dump!"

"So it's pretty yucky. Well, orphans don't get many choices," I said.

"Oh lose the drama, Sam. We're not orphans."

"Wanna bet?"

"Don't start that. Orphans go to orphanages or get adopted because they don't have parents, moron. I think if you look, Mom's in the kitchen cleaning cupboards."

"I'll find the dictionary and show you, as soon as we get unpacked." And I did too, showing her in the dictionary that a child who loses one parent can also be called an orphan.

"You'll see, Humpy. Orphan or not, when you go to school next year you won't be the tallest kid or the fastest runner or anything. You'll just be another stupid freshman in a big school. And I'll be that junior girl that nobody knows or wants to." She stomped off with a pair of boxes and disappeared through the dirty green door that led to our new home.

The sky was suddenly full of noise, and I looked up to see a trio of fighter jets roaring in low to land at the air force base. It was amazing to see real jets flying just above my head like the ones on the model airplane boxes. It wasn't long though, after the flash and roar, that the ribbons of exhaust across the sky became just part of the incessant noise. Distant thunder behind the storm of cars, kids, and trains.

Our new home was a two-bedroom apartment on the second floor. Five rooms with white walls: a kitchen with an electric stove; a complete bathroom glistening with porcelain and chrome; two bedrooms and a living room with windows that opened to let the musty air escape.

My room had a window with a view of the gravel and potholes of the parking lot. Beyond that was the natural hedge of cottonwoods and alders along the bluff, and beyond that the screech, chug, and whistle of the railroad yard that carried a hint of mystery and adventure. No room for snares or traplines, no snug hummocks where a boy could hide and daydream, but I had to admit that back home had no railroads, fighter jets, or playgrounds. Luckily, for the time being, the excitement of newness had me forgetting the leaving part of moving.

I had three boxes piled on the bed. One box was jeans, T-shirts, and underwear that I sorted into the bottom drawer of a metal refugee from an army barracks. It matched the single metal bed that took up most of the space. The room was small, but it was mine and the first time I'd had a room of my own. In the coming months it would become a refuge from all things that weren't.

The other boxes were the important ones. One was a Black

Label Beer case. The bottom was reinforced with tape and packed so full of comics that I barely made it up the stairs without a rest. Half of the comics made a neat stack on the corner of the bureau; the rest went under the bed.

One box remained, a Smirnoff Vodka case with bottle dividers in place. One by one I removed the models packed in newspaper, slowly rolling the paper out in my hand like these were the last Christmas gifts under the tree. Each one had an importance that extended beyond the values of plastic models, glued and painted piece by piece.

There had been tough choices when I packed my things in Ninilchik. Mom gave me one box for my books and models, and I'd had to sort through boxes of treasures to find pieces that meant something, that would help me remember. Everything else went into two other boxes, one for things to give away and one to be stored in the attic of the cabin to wait for the day I returned. I could only believe that all of this was just temporary.

My plastic models that made the cut were a Ford station wagon, an X-15 rocket plane, and a Corvette convertible. The others were glue-stained or missing parts, so I put them on the closet shelf. The X-15 and the 1965 Corvette I lined up on the windowsill. The Corvette was from Becky, when she drew my name for the class gift exchange. I kept it to help me remember her. The rocket plane had been a birthday gift from Dad, the last, I realized. Now all I had were these pieces of plastic and paint and a strange sick feeling when I thought of them.

The Ford station wagon with wood grain trim was just like the car we had taken Dad in to the hospital when he had his first heart attack. When I set it in place on the bureau—a new place in a new room—I felt a warm knot in my throat.

Once we settled in our apartment, it became a home without a mother. Each day, Mom was up by five, showered, and sitting at the table with a cup of coffee in her robe looking out the window before she dressed and caught the bus downtown. She worked at the big hotel there. She was a waitress until three then a hostess or cashier until closing. Most nights she didn't come home until ten. By then, she wanted her "sippin' and slippers": a short glass of whiskey and her sheepskin slippers. With those two comforts and a kiss from her kids she would sleep on the couch until it was time to start again.

There was no more fresh bread in the house. No hot stew with dumplings. The mother I'd had for all these years moved out and left her twin. This was a mother at work, going to work, home from work, or tired from work. She didn't make jelly and she bought Wonder Bread.

Mary and I had a list of chores for each day, including cleaning and laundry until finally, Mary even admitted we had become orphans. I determined to get along by doing anything I chose for as long as I could, undisturbed. I daydreamed and read my comics, and Mickey Spillane detective novels. I inherited Mickey Spillane from Joe, who didn't think I would understand them, but I did. Spillane wrote stories about tough-guy detectives, urban Tarzans taking on the rough jungle life of the city.

My third Sunday in Anchorage I lay with my feet propped up on the windowsill and a book under my nose. I was using up an afternoon helping Mike Hammer track a high society killer. Mom was running the vacuum up and down the hall in her weekend ritual of cleaning everything in the apartment, dirty or not. She was in her Sunday jeans and sweatshirt that she changed into after what Mary and I called "church shopping." We had been to three different churches in a month, and she still wasn't settled on one that fit her philosophy. This week she had walked out shaking her head. "What Bible has he been reading?" she asked in disgust. Mary and I just nodded and looked at each other.

She shut off the vacuum long enough to shout down the hall at me, but I pretended not to hear. Then I heard her footsteps coming to my room. She didn't share my literary convictions, so Spillane went under the bed and out came a book called *Touchdown Trouble*—sports stories were more to Mom's approval. She rapped on the door and followed that in.

She leaned on the doorjamb and glared. "Go and meet some of the kids in the neighborhood," she said. "You'll never make friends sitting in here with your nose in a book."

"I don't want to meet anybody." I threw my book facedown on the rumpled bedspread.

"You don't mean that. Go on outside."

"One more chapter?"

"You can finish the chapter you're on. That's all."

More arguments would just start a fight, so I read until she finished vacuuming and jumped me again. "I thought I told you to go outside."

"You did. I'm going." Then I stomped down the stairs into a cold, cloudy Anchorage June.

The only kids out and about in the neighborhood were three little girls playing on a rusty swing set. I roamed down the block away from the dreary apartment building and onto a street full of small houses. Mom was right. I wanted, perhaps desperately, to have friends, but meeting strangers seemed like a much-too-difficult way to do it. These people already had friends and lives. They didn't need me.

How did a guy make friends? I was born with all mine, or

they rolled into town and took up with the rest of the kids in school. I came from a place where friends were the kids you grew up with, like brothers and sisters almost, some you loved, some you hated, but, at sometime or another, you played with them all. Back home was too far away now, so I put it out of my mind.

I daydreamed I was playing tight end for a football team and trying to win the big one all by myself. My team was the underdog, and rain had turned the field to mud. I scooped up a fumble and ran, dodging, twisting, and turning through the stumbling tacklers of the other team.

Out of nowhere, a real football soared by me, nearly beaning me just before it bounced off the hood of a Plymouth station wagon. I stumbled after the ball and carried it back to a gang of kids in the middle of the street.

"Wanna play some touch?" a tall skinny teenager asked. "We need another guy."

"Sure," I said, a little nervous.

I was tall for my age, so the two teams argued over who deserved most to benefit from my obvious size and possible skill. I ended up with a short boy with a pug nose they called Macek and his bigmouthed pal, Taylor. I told them I could play tight end, which from my book-only experience meant I ran down the field and caught passes for touchdowns.

We formed a three-cornered huddle. Taylor squinted like a tough guy. "You catch a pass?" he asked.

"You bet. Just get it to me," I answered with a line right out of *Touchdown Trouble*.

"Good, 'cause we're three touchdowns behind."

Taylor puffed up. "Okay, do a quick block and sprint down the middle of the street."

For the first time in my life I took my place on the line of scrimmage. The skinny teenager lined up across from me and when Taylor said "HIKE!" he tried to push me over, but I moved to the side and dashed down the street, turning just in time to see the ball sail far to my left and once more bounce off a car.

Back in the huddle, Taylor glared at me like I was supposed to catch anything he threw. "Sorry," I said.

Little pug nose chimed in. "Get it to him this time, Taylor. I'll block."

I never got a look at the ball that hit me in the back of the head, and on the next play Taylor never saw the tag that got him before he could move. He stood panting in the huddle. His face was flushed bright red behind a spatter of freckles.

"You guys gotta block this time," he growled.

"Yeah," said Macek, "throw me the ball."

Once more we gained no yards but I got my block, paying for it with scraped knees. The kid named Taylor growled some more, "You guys aren't trying. We can beat these guys."

We only allowed the skinny high schooler and his team two more touchdowns before parents started appearing at the doors of the houses calling the boys home. Soon, only Macek, Taylor, and I stood awkwardly in the middle of the street.

Macek was short and stocky with a brown crew cut. Taylor was nearly as tall as I was, with a pile of red hair to match his freckles. "So, you just move here or something?" he asked.

"Yeah, from Ninilchik, down on the peninsula."

"You're from *Chickenshit*?" Macek said. He laughed.

I laughed, too. "No, Na-nil-chik!"

"My dad took me fishin' there once," Taylor said. "It's out in the boonies. I caught lots of king salmon there."

"In the boonies with the loonies!" Macek added. Only he laughed this time and I winced.

I tried to picture Taylor on the banks of the Ninilchik River in a sweatshirt and hip boots, trudging out from his dad's camper with a salmon rod in his hand. Maybe last summer, Harry and I had sold him some of the lures we salvaged from the snags in the river. Maybe we'd go this summer, Taylor and his dad and me, and I could show them where to catch the big ones and the places where the snags could steal your hooks.

"Where do you live now?" Macek asked.

"Hollywood Arms, those big green apartments across Hollywood Drive. We're on the top floor."

"Now there's a dump for you. My dad calls it the ghetto."

I was surprised at him talking that way, even if I didn't know exactly what a ghetto was. "It's not like I get to choose where I live."

"Yeah, well you better watch out. 'Cause them people got nothin' and they'll rob ya blind. That's what my dad says."

Taylor jumped to my defense. "Your dad just says that. He's never even been in those apartments."

"Yeah and he wouldn't be either."

"You're a jerk," Taylor said, "and your dad doesn't know crap."

"Sure he does. He knows you!" Macek said. He was chomping on a wad of bubblegum and the juice bubbled out when he talked. He laughed.

"I know you are but what am I?" Taylor returned.

"Where do you guys live?" I asked, interrupting their silly argument.

"Mr. Know-It-All lives way down past the shopping center, and I live right there," said Taylor, pointing to a blue house with a garage and chain-link fence. "Heck, we lived in the Spruce Tree Courts when we first moved here, and it was just as bad as the Arms. My dad kept having to go yell at the neighbors to quit playin' their music so loud. He'd have kicked their butts if they had the guts to fight him."

Silently, I thanked Taylor for getting me out of that one. I'd never had to fight a total stranger before, even though Macek didn't look like he would be much of a fight. It would be a fearful sort of encounter without any kind of relationship to fall back on when it was over. I always thought hitting a stranger would be easier than a good friend like Harry, but it didn't seem to work that way.

To think I was going to tell them how cool it was to live in an apartment, on the second floor yet, and we were going to get TV. Now I find out it's not cool at all. I suddenly envied Macek and Taylor for their yards and houses and dads to tell them things, though I couldn't remember my father ever telling me rotten things like that about other people.

I risked an invitation, "You guys want to come over and play on the bluff behind the apartments tomorrow? The alders are neat and we can climb around and stuff." How bold I felt to invite, to assume, friendship with two guys I'd just met.

"I'm spendin' the night at Macek's here, so yeah, why not? If Macek isn't afraid someone will rob him." We laughed and Macek slugged Taylor in the shoulder.

I left my new-found pals to finish their fight alone and ran all the way home. I had found some friends, but the apartment looked shabby and worn out. Did I imagine faces glaring at me from every window? The three little girls I had seen earlier were still on the swings and I observed that two were black and one brown. I hadn't noticed before.

A guilty relief filled me when I found a little white girl with a jack-o-lantern grin perched on the steps. She was dirty and lean, a deserted runt on the front porch. I smiled when she said hello and tried not to let her know that I was staring at her forehead. It was impossible not to stare: a lump stuck out of her forehead just above her eyes. The strangest nodule of skin and tissue that I had ever seen jutted from her head like a misplaced navel. A giant mole? No, more like a belly button, one that stuck out instead of in. She had an "outie" right in the middle of her forehead.

I climbed the steps refusing to look back, though I wanted to stare and even touch the weird magnetic oddness of it. Never in my life had I seen such an astonishing curiosity on anyone's face. I announced it when I walked in the door. "Did you see that little girl with the belly button on her head?"

"Samuel!" Mom was stretched on the couch with a stack of official papers on her chest, looking tired and lonely.

"Well, Mom, she does."

"I'm aware of that, but don't you think it's cruel to make fun of her?" Then her tone changed. "I can't believe her mother can't have that thing removed."

"They live upstairs," offered Mary, dancing to the radio as she set the tiny table for three. "Her mom's a drunk, and worse, I bet."

"Where on earth did you hear such a thing?"

"Mom, you can hear everything in this place. The way that woman talks, you better stuff cotton in Humpy's ears when he goes to bed."

"His name is Sam, and that will be just enough of that. I expect you to treat that little girl nicely. She has enough to put up with without you two giving her a bad time. Get in there and put supper on the table."

Supper was still strange with just three of us, but no one mentioned it. Instead we looked beyond the room for topics. "Mom, why do all these Negroes live here?" I asked around a mouthful of chicken. Back in Ninilchik I'd never seen but two black people before and now they were all around me. I didn't say so, but they scared me a little.

"They're just people," asserted Mom.

"One of them talked to me today," Mary said.

"That's nice," Mom answered tersely. "You just stay away from them."

"But I was down at the laundry room," Mary continued, "and this lady came in and got her sheets out of the dryer. She just asked me where I was from and stuff like that."

"I didn't say they weren't friendly. I just said stay away. They have their life and we have ours. Now get after those dishes." Mom left us with no chance for questions and went off to her bath.

I went to bed filled with images of that little girl with the belly button on her forehead. Maybe her mom was a witch who practiced black magic on helpless children. Maybe she wasn't a little girl at all but a bat, or a unicorn changed by some trick of magic. After all, it was nighttime when I saw her.

The way Mom talked about our neighbors managed to make this place even more mysterious. The smells of cooking food and sounds of music coming from the other apartments were as foreign as any I could imagine. From the mold, the mildew, and the accented voices of the hallways, to the unfamiliar spicy food odors and pounding, pounding music that leaked through open windows, I was surrounded by this strange and sinister place that I must call home. I was glad it was summer so the night wasn't dark.

Chapter 5

Mom always made us get up before she went to work, so I had time to write a letter before I went to the bluff to meet my new friends. I lay on the bed with the remains of my Big Chief writing tablet and wrote "Dear Becky."

"I'm fine," I wrote. "Hope you are too." I chewed on my pencil. Then I went to the kitchen and poured a glass of milk. This was my first letter to a girl, and I was at a loss for words. What could I say that really mattered? I didn't want to say too much and be mushy, or not say anything and have her stop being my girlfriend.

I was losing my mental picture of Becky, and I wondered what it was that I liked about her. In my top drawer was the scented, flowered note card with Becky's address. I dug it out and laid it on the bed to let the fading perfume work on me.

I took a half hour to say that we had moved into an apartment and that summer was boring here just like at home. I couldn't tell her the secrets, the mysteries that abounded in this foreign place. I was too proud to say much about how I missed climbing the alders on the bluff and building forts with my friends back home. Instead I told her to write and say hi to people and gave up. The letter went in an envelope and into the drawer with Dad's cribbage board. Maybe I could mail it in a few days. But suddenly I didn't want to.

Becky and Harry Munson, all the kids that had been a part of me, were receding on the tide of my life, and I feared that soon they would be too far away to reach.

I ran all the way to the bluff. There were birds out, and I spooked a squirrel that chattered and screamed against my right to be there. Below me at the base of the steep hill train cars moved back and forth, squealing their brakes and clanging as they met. I could just see pieces and colors through the branches and leaves, but the scene seemed dirtier and more confusing than the train sets I'd seen in people's basements or in Western movies.

I wandered along the bicycle trail with its humps and rolls and wished I had a bike, one with a banana seat and high handlebars.

I heard a clatter and turned to watch a bike approaching. It was a bike like I had just been thinking about, and I knew by the sound that the owner had clipped a playing card to the frame so that it hit the spokes, imitating an engine, a dream of power. The rider was slim and dark haired. He was sleek like the bike and they moved together, lightly touching the tops of the bumps and swerving around rocks and bushes. Twice the bike left the ground but the kid turned it and landed square on the trail. He stopped. Maybe because I was in the trail, but he stopped and smiled.

"How ya doin'?" I said in my boldest fashion.

"Hi."

"Nice bike."

"Thanks, I just got it. You got one?" His question, I realized in a moment of wondrous clarity, was an attempt at friendship, a probing for familiarity.

"No."

"I wanted a skateboard," he said, leaning on the handlebars, "but Gram said they're too dangerous. Sheesh!"

"My mom said the same thing," I lied. "Most fun things are that way."

"You want to try it?" He pushed the bike to me, and I saw his hands and arms were slim and delicate like a girl's. I nearly threw him off the bike and yanked it from him. Did I want to try it? Yes, yes, yes, yes!

"Sure," I said. "Oh yeah, my name's Hum—I mean Sam." I didn't want to chance another embarrassment about my nickname.

"Billy."

I took the handlebars and lifted the bike. It weighed nothing, like holding air, and the seat was hard and strange against my rump. Then I was flying, soaring along the dirt. First sitting, then standing, then rolling over a bump as if the bike were trying to run away from me into a dip. But at the dip I leaned back and the front wheel lifted off the ground. Over I went with the bike landing safely on top.

"All right! Way to go!" The voices weren't Billy's. The shame was mine.

"Cool bike, huh?" I said to the smiling Taylor and the leering Macek as they suddenly appeared behind us.

"Not bad," they said in unison.

Billy helped hide my embarrassment. "They're tricky to learn to ride on the bumps," he said. "I was crashing like crazy for a couple of days." I liked him for that.

"I knew that," Taylor said.

"Are you kidding?" said Macek. "They're a piece of cake." I smiled sickly and nodded.

"This is Billy," I said. I noticed he didn't offer them a try on his bike.

"Hey," the others replied.

And so, with the bike stashed in the weeds, we charged down the alder trees. Their long and limber trunks grew out nearly straight from the steep bluff, creating a combination of a tightrope and a trampoline. We ran leaping and springing from trunk to trunk, each one bouncier than the next. For just a little while, four kids dropped their guard and allowed themselves to be friends and play like little boys.

"You're it," I said pushing Taylor off balance and leaping to another branch. He quickly ran up a big trunk and tagged Macek off. "You're it!"

Macek tried forever to catch one of us, then Billy felt sorry for him and let himself be caught. He tagged Taylor in an instant and bounded lightly away. We all chased him, but he would slip away from us and run to the thin, limber ends of the trees, bending them to the ground and then leaping to another higher one. At last, we lost interest in my wild country sport, and we sat in a sunny spot between the branches, invisible from above.

"Know any jokes?" Taylor asked, his face sparkling with sweat and his eyes with mischief.

Macek couldn't resist. "What's green and hangs from the trees?"

"Everybody knows that. Elephant snot!" answered Taylor.

Billy laughed. "What's black and dangerous?"

"A gorilla with a machine gun!"

"No! A crow with diarrhea!"

It was time to raise the ante. It was time to use all the things I learned from Dean, the eighth grader who sat by me on the bus all through fifth grade and filled my ear with dirty jokes and cuss words. Dean who sat by me because the kids his age hated him, and the older kids, including his brother, would punch him if he went to the back of the bus. He sat by me and there found an audience for his crude jokes.

"Did you hear about this guy who was traveling cross-country and his car broke down?" I asked. The others leaned forward as I launched into the story. "He goes up to this farmhouse and says to the farmer, 'Can I stay the night?' 'Yeah, says the farmer, but you'll have to sleep with my daughter.'"

The guys laughed and bent closer as my voice dropped. "'Okay!'" says the guy, and the farmer takes him to his daughter's bedroom. The next morning they're having breakfast and the farmer says, 'Did you like my daughter?' 'Yeah,' says the guy. 'But every time I kissed her she spit rice in my face.'"

They laughed without knowing why.

"'Well,'" says the farmer, "'number one, that wasn't rice, and number two, she's been dead for six months.'"

"EEWWW!" they groaned and laughed. Except Taylor, who said, "I don't get it."

Macek blurted out, "Maggots!" Three of us laughed, hard.

All the filthy and disgusting stories we could muster poured out on the bluff and rustled among the dead alder leaves that day. We were wild and unchained and for the moment unbound by our age. It felt like we were outlaws hiding in the woods from the world and its grown-up rules.

"We need a fort!" declared Taylor suddenly, "a hideout, a place of our own where we can do whatever we want."

"This spot is good," said Macek. We were covered from every direction but above by the turn of the hill and canopy of alder. A wall of devil's club rose on straight stalks covered with tiny thorns.

"What are we, little kids?" Billy asked. "We don't need a fort, we need a *hangout*."

"That's what I meant. But there's always lots of little kids around here," complained Taylor, seeming to trust no one. "They'll get into our stuff or tell on us." I wondered what evil they had in mind.

"I know a place where nobody ever goes," said Billy, no longer the quiet member of our gang. "Over between the base and the houses where I live there's a gully that's all wild and bushy."

"I know what you mean," Macek interrupted. "That's down by my house."

"Oh, yeah!" said Taylor. "That would be perfect."

"But," said Macek, his voice turned sinister, "it's kinda scary. I heard they found a body there once."

I knew that trick. "Sounds great to me. Maybe Taylor can find a girl who spits rice."

We laughed again at Taylor's expense then we laid plans for the site in the gully until Taylor tired of dreaming and wanted action. "Come on," he ordered, and started down the hill through the brush. He headed for the railroad yard I had ogled that morning with curiosity and wonder. Trains were new enough to me, and the lure of just watching them come and go, hitch and uncouple, was enough to make me follow our self-proclaimed leader.

"Where we going?"

"Time for a raid!" said Taylor. He stopped in front of a chain-link fence that sagged pathetically into the weeds and an official metal sign that stated, "No Trespassing. Violators Will Be Prosecuted." I hung on the fence and stared up at a blue caboose that sat only feet away from the fence.

"It's not red," I said.

"What?" Taylor turned and looked stupidly into my face.

"The caboose, it's not red."

"None of them are."

"They're supposed to be red."

"Well, sorry about that. I'll tell the head engineer next time I see him. "Hey, guys. Mr. Samual Humpster from Nickelshit, Alaska, train capital of the world, says cabooses are supposed to be red." The barb hurt but I laughed, beating them to the punch.

"You really must be from the boondocks!" said Macek. "Ain't you ever seen a train?"

"Not up close. No railroads where I come from."

"Then you are in for a treat, because I'm giving you a personal tour of an official BLUE Alaska Railroad caboose."

Billy was startled, as I was. "We can't go in there," he said. "We'll get arrested."

"Well aren't we brave! You only get arrested if you get caught," chided Taylor, "and I'm not getting caught."

Billy winced and stuck his hands in his pockets. I was suddenly cold and feeling very far from home.

"Last one over the fence is a sissy!" whispered Taylor, and he was gone.

By the time I followed Billy over the settling chain link, Taylor and his shadow squatted by the steps to the caboose. It loomed like a great castle before me and I licked dry lips with a swollen tongue. The crunch of feet on gravel echoed against the colossal metal building that stood like a mountain beyond the tracks.

I remembered a tale I'd read of hobos chased by railroad cops who were giants with clubs the size of axe handles. They chased any hobos they found and beat them to death. I couldn't remember how many steps it was from the fence to the caboose, but I wanted to.

Taylor led us up the steps and tested the door. The platform was dirty and smelled of oil and the door was gray with soot and grime. Unlocked. We were in. It was dark and musty like it should have been, and for a moment I forgot my terrible conscience, allowing myself to taste the flavor of great machines and outlaw exploits. The four of us had crept through the jungle and taken possession of a train. We had bridled the iron horse.

"Let's get some flares!" We dug through toolboxes and closets for treasure, groping in the dark for long red sticks that looked like dynamite and promised the power of fire.

Then, out of the shadows reached the hand of authority and burst my bubble of fantasy. A rough, strong hand held my shoulder, then pulled me upright and turned me . . . turned my heart to mud, my knees to oatmeal, and my face toward a man in coveralls and a hard hat. No uniform or club, no gun, just a hand, a hard hat, and a question.

"What are you doing here?" asked the man. He had a face as black as midnight, and his eyes seemed to glow in the near darkness.

I saw three T-shirts flash through the door behind him and then they were gone. Free. I heard their feet on the gravel then the rattle of the fence. I searched for words, for escape. Like the hobos in the story, I saw myself lying in the cinders beside a train, wetting the rails with my blood. This was the hard fist of authority and that fist was meant to crush violators of signs that read, "No Trespassing. Violators Will Be Prosecuted."

"Just looking around," I said, trying to hold the flares out of sight.

"What are you doing with these?" He snatched them away, and I was glad, for just the guilt of having them made my hand burn.

"Nothing."

"You're in big trouble, kid. What's your name?" He loomed above me like a great bear about to devour me.

I needed a lie. It was the time and place. I needed it bad. The truth was quick and easy, but lies had to be planned and shaped, assembled like a model car, piece by piece. Lies take time, time I didn't have.

All of the sudden, Billy stuck his head in the door of the caboose, and his voice didn't even tremble. "We're brothers," he said. "He's Joey and I'm Frank." The lie was there like an angel at my shoulder.

The face, a black face like one I had never met before, rotated and examined Billy's very pale one. "This is a dangerous place. You kids should know better."

"Yessir."

"I ought to call your parents." Gruesome previews of my mother's anger and disappointment became a great sour ball in my mouth.

"Yessir."

"Now get outta here. If I catch you here again, I'm calling the cops." I felt the kindness in him and knew he was lying now. With the passing of my panic, I saw a face that wanted to laugh, that didn't want to scare boys gone exploring, a face that wanted to run with us up through the fireweed and devil's club under the sweeping alders.

"Yessir!"

By the time we reached the back of the apartment we could laugh. We had taken an incredible and dangerous journey and had now returned safe but not unmarked. We were different. I could feel the newness of seeing a part of myself that I had never seen, and as we wandered across and out of the parking lot that was my backyard, we were quiet, each looking with curiosity into the hole where fear lived with panic and terror. Not the childish scary notion that we might be grounded, or spanked, or yelled at, but honest, raw fear of irrevocable violence from strangers without guilt. Only by some crazy luck, in our view, had we found a for-giver, a man with compassion.

That day we made an amazing discovery, the kind that changes you forever. Yes, we had been caught and scared, but we had also gotten away with it. We had uncovered a powerful secret: Trespassers are *not* always prosecuted.

Chapter 6

Several days after the raid on the railroad yard, I made my way down Hollywood Drive and across Bluff Road to a neighborhood of small houses where Billy lived. He brought his bike and we headed down his street with no destination in mind. We were nomads. Free from supervision, chores, or other activities devised by adults.

"Don't you just hate it?" Billy said. "They tell us when to wake up and they tell us when to eat and what."

"Yeah, my mom still reminds me to go pee. Like I might forget. And every day there's a chore list. Mom leaves it on the table every morning, like the newspaper."

Billy was quiet for moment. "In a way I'm lucky, I guess. No chores. Not many anyway." Then his voice changed, got low and serious. "Actually, I don't even have a mom right now. Not here anyway."

"Really?" I looked around like someone might be listening.

"Yeah, she and my dad split up and she went off to California to 'get her head together,' whatever that means."

"I'm sorry, man. That stinks." Now it was my turn to sound serious. "I know how that is. My dad isn't coming back ever."

"Yeah, Macek told me. He said you told him you were an orphan, but he said you aren't."

"When one parents dies you *are* an orphan," I argued. "I looked it up."

Billy chuckled and I glared at him, wondering what was amusing. "Sorry, it just sounds funny, you looking it up. You must be some kind of bookworm who does good in school."

"Used to be."

"Not me. It's all I can do to keep out of the special class. I guess it's 'cause I been to so many schools with us moving a lot. And now I'm here at my gramma's while my dad's overseas."

"Overseas? Where? Is he a soldier?"

"He's in Vietnam and he's a soldier so he's gotta go. Works on a helicopter—that part's cool."

"That would be cool, being in a real battle and all."

"Yeah, but I wish he was here."

"I bet," I said, a little envious of a guy who could look forward to his dad coming home. "You'll make friends here. Heck, we'll do it together. And this school year, we'll be big shot ninth graders—you and me."

"If I'm still here."

"Of course you'll be here. You gotta help me. It's going to be totally different for me. Last year I was in a class with fifteen kids, can you believe it? Central Junior High must have like a hundred freshman."

"That'll be cool. If we are not in jail." We both laughed, but I felt a chill. Our walk had taken us to a street that ran by the woods above the railroad yard and scene of our raid. I felt self-conscious out in the open so close to the scene of the crime.

"That guy was scary, huh? The guy in the railroad yard."

Billy leaned on his handlebars. "Just a guy. Really big though. He had you pretty spooked, didn't he?" Then he was kind and added, "I was spooked too, but I couldn't just leave you there."

"I was scared, I gotta say, he could have got me good. I had the flares in my hand and everything. My mom would have beat my ass for sure."

Billy nodded. "Yeah, it sounds like your mom takes things pretty serious."

"That she does." I was going to tell him why I thought that guy was scary and why I was so frozen. I wanted to tell him, get it off my chest, but suddenly, Billy launched into action. He swung onto his bike and dropped off the sidewalk onto a rough trail down a shallow dip and into a gravel parking lot full of potholes. I watched Billy descend and bounce through the bumps then across a driveway, behind a building, and then reappear on the opposite side. He had to pump like crazy up a trail that brought him back to the finish panting and smiling.

"Try it," he said, pushing the bike to me.

The same confidence that took me into the railroad yard carried me over the crest of the hill. After the first bump though, confidence deserted me, and I no longer rode the bike; we just shared the same path. Even then, for a long brave moment, I thought it would be fine. The turn at the building was my demise. I parted with the bike and skidded across the gravel on my forearm, arriving on my face at the front door of a low, wide building.

Concrete is harder and asphalt messier, but for scar-making, meat-grinding bodily harm, there is nothing like using your bare forearm for a brake when falling off a speeding bike in a gravel parking lot. I screamed.

Billy got down that hill nearly as fast as I did. He came, I supposed, to kick my butt for wrecking his bike for the second time. Panting, he leaned over with his hands on his knees. "Shit! Are you okay?"

My right arm had a few scrapes and hurt like fire, but my left arm was bleeding through the gravel and dirt where a patch of skin the size of my palm had been scoured away. "I'm okay," I moaned, picking the larger bits of gravel out of my arm. I could feel the tears leaving tracks through the dirt on my cheeks.

Billy didn't seem to notice. "Boy, can you yell!" he said. "Are you hurt bad? Do you want to go home?"

"No. Sorry if I scared you. And sorry about your bike, too. Again," I replied, shaking my foolish head. I had to get my mind off my aching arm. I looked up from the ground and there was a pair of double doors with a fancy awning staring back at me. Instantly, something clicked in my head. It seemed that everywhere I turned in this new neighborhood, there was something new and different, something fat with invitation.

Even with blood running down my arm, I wanted to get up and walk right through those doors.

Billy retrieved his bike and checked it for damage. "The bike's no problem. Can you walk and everything?"

"Yeah, sure." I stared at the building looming above me. Its doors were carved with a bull caribou and straps of black iron ran across the door from the hinges, but the iron door handle was chained and padlocked. Alone in the middle of this giant gravel lot, the building squatted, dark and mysterious. And it called to me like a mountain to be climbed.

"That building looks cool. Let's check it out," I said to Billy.

"What?" The look he gave me was filled with questions, but he kept them to himself and followed me across the trackless lot.

"This is the Caribou Club," he explained, "but it never opened. It was a really weird deal. There were advertisements for a big grand opening with a band and all that stuff, but then the earthquake hit and it just never opened."

We walked the full circumference of the place, wading through dandelions to peek into painted windows. We kicked at bottles, poked in the weeds, and pulled hopelessly at locked doors.

"Doesn't anyone ever come here?" I asked. My arm was no longer hurting; it just ached, and the building was drawing me in.

"Nobody. See for yourself. There aren't even any car tracks." Billy was right. Here sat a building surrounded by houses, people, and cars, but it was left completely alone. Inspiration came when I causally tried the knob at the back door. The knob turned and the door started to open but was stopped by a padlock.

"Wait a minute," said Billy, pointing at the lock. "Check that out."

The padlock was in place, but it wasn't closed. Someone had left it unlocked, just for us, just for fun. With the reverence that such luck deserves my hand closed around the lock and I let my weight hang against it. I was suddenly too tired to take the next step. My head was beginning to ache. It was too soon.

"Tomorrow," I said, "we'll go in together." Billy just smiled and nodded.

The magic of the place was strong, but I was feeling hot and woozy after my fall, too weak and unprepared for another adventure. Tomorrow. Tomorrow would be soon enough, after I had dreamed up the mystery of the place.

We were walking home along Hollywood Drive when I had the courage to tell the truth. "Sorry about your bike. You know, I haven't actually ridden much."

"No kidding? How could I tell?" We shared a laugh as Billy imitated my crazy downhill ride. The world was suddenly brighter.

The next day, our trip back to the Caribou Club was delayed when we joined up with Macek and Taylor, something I hadn't done since the incident at the railroad yard. I wasn't sure how to react to them running off like they did, or getting me in that fix in the first place. But when Macek showed up at my door and begged me to hang out with them, I couldn't resist.

Unlike where Macek lived, the streets in Taylor's neighborhood were curbless and unpaved. Instead of rows of similar houses centered on green lawns, here it seemed like a giant broom swept up the big and small houses and scattered them onto untidy lawns along Bluff Road. Taylor's family lived here with the other air force families who could find homes only a mile from the base.

We were supposed to meet at a vacant lot that was Taylor's hangout. The lot, it turned out, was not vacant at all, but contained a collapsed fence, a ton of garbage, and a Quonset hut that sat in the middle of the weeds like an elephant with a broken back. A wall of alders created a barrier from the road, and I was several yards into the lot before I could actually see the worn-out army shelter. A Quonset hut was a ready-made building used by the army all over Alaska. It had a curved roof that went to the ground to form walls, so it looked like a Quaker Oats canister cut in half.

Gray plywood covered the windows and the door didn't latch. It was propped closed with a stick.

My new friends were hiding in the hut and leaped out with the *da-da-da-da-da-dat* of machine-gun fire.

"Nice try, suckers. Boy, are you scary!" I jeered.

"Where you been?" demanded Macek, posing like a military officer in cutoffs.

"Had some things to do."

"Well gosh, we been waiting forever."

"Well, speaking of things to do, you two sure were brave soldiers at the railroad yard," I returned in a volley to Macek and Taylor.

"Just 'cause you were dumb enough to stand around and get caught," chided Taylor.

"Yellowbellies!" I answered.

Taylor made a fist and stuck out what chest he had, ready to defend honor that he didn't have. Billy, who seemed to save his words for emergencies, saved all of us from having to fight. "You guys were lucky you ran when you did. That guy was a monster. I thought he was going to eat us alive."

He threw me a bone too. "Yeah, that guy was B-I-G big! Sam stood right up to him though. The guy says 'What are you doin' here?' and Ol' Sam looks innocent as pie and says, 'Just lookin' around'." He patted me on the back while he laughed. He had the other two with him by then. "'Just lookin' around' he says when he's got a handful of flares."

I took the lead. "And this guy was so dumb," I heard myself say, "when he asks me my name I'm chokin', ya know, and Billy goes, 'He's Joey and I'm Frank; we're brothers.' It was great." The two of us laughed, remembering our fear.

Macek traded his anger for fascination. "Then what happened? Did he call the cops?"

Taylor wasn't impressed, or was he jealous? "They don't call the cops on kids, you twerp."

"Naw, he just yelled at us and we said 'Yessir' a zillion times and split."

"Speaking of splitting, let's go. I've only got a couple of hours," said Billy, and we were off to the new hangout in the gully. Macek tried to make a smart remark, but Taylor pushed him into the weeds and charged down the path that led us behind the Quonset hut and down into the woods. We gave up on the Quonset hut because it had too many kids who knew about it to be a good hangout for us. Even high schoolers sometimes went there to drink beer and neck with girls.

Billy and I hung back behind the others, and I kept thinking about the man in the railroad yard, and what I hadn't told Billy before. "I never met a Negro before," I told him.

Billy was caught by surprise. "You what?"

"The guy in the railroad caboose. . . . I never met a Negro before."

"Really?" he said, grinning. "Well, that's no big deal. I know lots of black people and they're just people. Except for one thing: don't call them Negroes. They are called Blacks. Have you ever met a Mexican before?"

"Don't think so."

"Well meet one now!" he said looking up to make sure the other boys didn't hear. "*I'm* half Mexican."

I gaped at him and all I could say was, "Cool."

We reached the gully, and as soon as we looked down into it I was sure. It was like the places I found along the bluff at Ninilchik where the steep bank was notched by a stream and filled with fallen trees and weeds. This spot was wider and even had some larger spruce trees sticking up out of the tangled alder, roses, and elderberry bushes. Partway down, the trail disappeared and we walked into a wall of devil's club.

I took the lead, proud to show my backwoods skill. Rather than try to climb around the prickly barriers, I stomped on the base of a stalk, pushing one tall plant over onto several others. And so, step by step, I proceeded to tramp a path through the weeds.

Gone were the road and the city that had imprisoned us. We had entered a jungle and become great explorers. I wished for a machete to help my explorer image. I grabbed a stick instead and slashed bravely at the cow parsnip stalks that rose higher than my head.

The mosquitoes were a reality that couldn't be ignored, however, and I stopped to pull a tiny jar of mosquito repellent from my pocket; I had come prepared. My companions cheered but soon found what I had already known: nothing would hold off mosquitoes forever.

Luckily we broke out into the sunlight by the creek and the host of mosquitoes resigned themselves to short forays out of their shaded bushes. A chunk of old metal roofing lay half in the creek. We decided to use the roofing to build a lean-to between two trees and cover that with brush for camouflage.

"First, everybody has to bring some food so we can eat down here when we want," said Billy. He didn't look it, but he was a serious eater who took it personally if an hour passed without a snack. Macek voted for soda pop and comics. Taylor and I argued that first we needed some building materials.

"I saw some electric company stuff up by the road," I volunteered. "There were some cross planks. You know those boards that fit on the top of power poles. They're just waiting for us." It took the better part of two hours, but we managed to get six of them down the hill and stacked next to the metal roofing. By then starvation had set in, and Billy had to get home so we climbed the hill, taking a second path in order to have an escape route.

We came out on the road tired, hungry, and dirty, and I wished I had enough money to go to the Big G Drive-In for a root beer and a sundae. I hardly noticed when Billy left. He went quietly, a little embarrassed at having to check in at home, but the others were too tired to razz him, and I was too sympathetic.

Then I had an idea and called after him, "Wait up, Billy!" I broke into a run.

All day I had been thinking about the Caribou Club. That great empty building waiting to be explored. I couldn't shake the nearly sinister fascination that it held for me. Perhaps I hit my head in the bike wreck and woke up like a newborn goose, imprinting on the first thing I saw, or maybe the forlorn aspect of something so neglected touched my sense of empathy, like the little girl in my apartment building with her belly button forehead.

The gully was remote and filled with mosquitoes and reminded me of home, but the Caribou Club was new and mysteriously exotic. I wanted to make it mine like nothing else was in this world of teenagers with cars and adults with power. If I could have the Caribou Club, "No Trespassing" would protect me. I'd already be inside. Away from the bugs in the gully, my spirits were revived, and it was time for action.

"Let's go to the club today," I said, catching up to Billy. I tried to be casual.

"You mean the Caribou?"

"Yeah!"

"What about the other guys?"

"Just you and me first. Got a flashlight?"

"Yeah." I could see the idea was growing in his mind. "I'll see ya in about an hour. At the gas station."

I was sitting on the curb watching for fancy Mustangs when

Billy trotted up with a green military-looking flashlight clipped to his belt. "You should have seen the cool Mustang that just came by," I said. "Jet black, chrome wheels. What a beauty."

"Any Corvette Stingrays?" he asked. "That's my favorite car." He stared hopefully down the hill at the string of pickups, station wagons, and sedans that rushed into sight around the corner. I shook my head, but he didn't see, he just grabbed my arm and pointed at a Corvette, direct from the future, gliding past in a flash of burgundy and silver. And as he turned his head to follow its path, I saw it reflected in his eyes, a burgundy ghost passing across the mirror of his soul.

"Let's go," I said. Today wasn't for Corvettes, Mustangs, or Chevy Nomads. We were headed for unexplored territory. There was a concrete reality that waited for the two of us in the building in the weeds.

We walked the long way around the ball field and approached the club from the alders in back, stepping quickly to the door and in without hesitation or breath. Once across the threshold of temptation, we froze. The building was cold, dark, and it swallowed us, as if the metal door was the clamping jaw of a great beast that had risen from the muddy waters of Cook Inlet and gobbled us up.

Our fear was no longer fear of getting caught. It was fear of the dark and the unknown, fear made bigger by our imagination. The black, the mystery, the building itself, all held our total attention so completely that there was no room to even recognize that we had actually once more crossed the line labeled "No Trespassing. Violators Will Be Prosecuted."

Unmoving, we waited together in the darkness that slowly grew to a weak twilight as our eyes adjusted to the bits of light that filtered through the boarded-up windows.

"Come on, amigo," I said bravely, "let's see what we've got."

"Roger Wilco," said my partner, and we flooded the hallway with light from our flashlights. Before us stretched a long hall without doors or windows, its floor covered with paper and crushed boxes. Beyond, a curtain of false night challenged our lights and shortened our strides. We crept. Attempted silence.

The floor was tile and our shoes refused to whisper, and instead announced our progress no matter how we moved them. Shuffling scattered the papers, making them rattle like dried leaves. Walking on tiptoe made our sneakers squeak and clomp. "Why are we sneaking?" Billy asked.

"I don't know."

We crept on.

Suddenly the darkness dissolved. Before us opened the mouth of a room so large that it threatened to swallow our tiny lights and us. We shrank back and swung our beams to the corners, roof, and far wall, creating dancing shadows that filled the cavern with bat-like motion. "Something's in here!" I whimpered.

"No! Just us. Wait! Hold your light still."

I heard Billy breathing, heavy like I had at the railroad yard. Our four eyes followed the path of light across the expanse, where something, someone, moved; a shadowed spirit-like breathing movement that beckoned us across the canyon of silence.

"Who's there?" challenged Billy, in a voice drained of confidence yet loud enough to echo in this grand canyon of mystery.

How small I felt next to such bravado. How weak and small beside Billy's booming voice.

"What's a matter?" he called to the darkness, "you chicken?" now fuller and stronger in resonance, confidence. As if draped in some powerful armor, Billy lead me through the shadows in an enchanted forest, sweeping back and forth with the blade of his lamp. The light opened a path through the mystery before us, and the motion we had detected grew bolder and more real.

When the beams of our lamps revealed a rumpling curtain that waffled in some breath of wind from the open door, we burst into laughter. The curtain ran along the wall behind a bandstand and I ran forward and swatted the curtain. The motion made it whisper and sweep away and then back into our faces, making us shiver and laugh again.

Parked comfortably on the bandstand, we played a game with the lights against the ceiling, walls, and floor. Then we saw for the first time that the floor was covered with blank restaurant receipts spread about as far as we could see into the unexplored shadows of our stronghold.

"Somebody's beat us to it," I observed.

"Yes we have!" snarled Billy in his scariest voice, and I turned to face him and jumped back at the specter. Billy had the flashlight held beneath his face so that it shown grotesquely on his open mouth and squinting eyes.

"You jerk!" I lunged for him, and he fled into the unknown with me at his back waving frantically with my flashlight. Without knowing it we entered another room through a great door. I tackled him in the sea of papers, where we rolled like fighting cats, kicking and shouting obscenities until we bumped against a restaurant counter or bar.

We raised ourselves by the legs of stools bolted to the floor and leered over the counter behind our lights. We each sat on a padded stool, and I imagined ordering from a pair of young beauties in uniforms of red and white with short skirts that showed their legs.

"Hey, sweetie, give me a double burger with cheese and a milkshake."

"Make mine a malted and a BLT."

"Wouldn't it be great? To have your own restaurant?" Billy said.

"To have your own waitress. No bossy high school kids, no parents," I added.

"Don't wish that."

"What?" Then I realized what I'd said, realized that I'd forgotten that I had lost one parent, remembered that it wasn't a game.

"It's not that cool. Trust me," Billy said.

My mouth was wide open but I closed it before my foot got there. Through the eerie light, Billy's face chilled me, the way it seemed to fade and shimmer like the curtains behind the bandstand. I passed over my curiosity and chose a different angle. "Well, should we let Taylor and Macek in on the action?"

"Why not? There's a whole stage for Macek to make an ass of himself on."

"Yeah and Taylor can be the bartender or bouncer."

"If they can keep their big mouths shut. Morons."

We sat at the counter, spinning on the stools and making fun of our friends until the batteries ran down in our flashlights. We hurried out into the daylight to call our friends and convince them to abandon the gully forever.

My dreams on the walk home were filled with lights and parties and sleepovers at a new Caribou Club with its floors swept clean. A place to play cards and listen to music where no one but us was in charge.

Chapter 7

Billy and I planned to spring our idea of the Caribou Club on Macek and Taylor at a backyard sleepover. Three of us set up a tent in Taylor's backyard where we had convinced our parents we would spend the night, and waited for Billy to get back from his check-in. "God, that guy can't get away to do anything," observed Taylor, who never seemed to have anyone at home to answer to.

"He's just not a very good liar," said Macek.

"Are you?" I asked, seriously wanting to understand this exacting science.

"Are you kidding? Right now my mom thinks that we're all going to sleep out in this tent so we can get enough experience to join Boy Scouts. And, she thinks the tent is at Billy's, not here at Taylor's."

Taylor and I both looked incredulous. "I make it a point to never tell my mom the truth about where I'm going and what I'm up to. That way there is never any doubt that I can pull off a big lie if I need to."

"What if she catches you?"

"Then I tell another lie. That's when parents least expect you to lie, see, when you've just been caught in one. The whole trick is to tell them what they want to hear, not some dumb excuse."

We shook our heads, I with disbelief and Taylor with sheer awe.

Billy brightened my mood when he trotted up the driveway with a six-pack of Coke under his arm. "Look what my gramma gave me. She said we ought to make a party of it."

How could you lie to a lady like that?

Dinner at Taylor's was bologna sandwiches and soup slurped up at the kitchen table while Taylor's mom watched TV. We gulped and bolted to the green gulley. I hadn't told the others about the Caribou Club. I had been eager at first. Even that morning, I had carried the story on the front of my tongue, rehearsing the sales pitch I would give for making that our hangout. But faced with the excitement of two of my new and possibly fragile friendships, I relented. There would be a right time.

When we finished the lean-to in the gully it was just big enough for the four of us to lie down in. I cut alders to close the open front of the shelter while Taylor and Bill worked with a big sheet of plastic we "discovered" in the alley behind an empty house. The lean-to was dark and cold, but no one admitted it. Instead we each shared our dreams to make it larger and fancier.

"At home we had the backseat from a car in our tree fort," I bragged.

"Right," said Taylor, "you hauled a big heavy car seat up in a tree. If you're going to be as good a liar as me, you better do better than that."

"Yeah, my brother helped me," I said. "I bet we could get

something like that down here. There's a ton of old junky cars in this neighborhood."

"If we have food, this place won't be so bad," said Taylor.

"There's still the bugs. This place is mosquito heaven." I decided right at that moment it was to time go with the Caribou Club.

"Food? Bugs? Who cares," said Macek. "I brought the good stuff." From his pocket he pulled a pack of Camels, which were so bent that pulling one complete cigarette from the pack would be impossible.

"Why don't you just run over them with a car next time, moron," chided Taylor. He pulled a pack of matches from his pocket and accepted a broken half of a filterless cigarette.

Taylor lit up first, puffing boldly with smoke billowing up into his eyes. We all laughed and coughed as he danced around the tiny hut with a burnt lip.

When he offered me one, I said, "Those gave my dad a heart attack. No thanks."

They all froze and stared at me.

"That must have been something," said Billy.

"Your dad had a heart attack?" Macek asked. "I thought cigarettes only give you cancer."

"They're bad for your heart too. My dad had two heart attacks, and the second one killed him." I'd never said it out loud before and it surprised me.

"Were you there, you know, when it happened?" asked Macek.

"I was there for his first one," I answered, and suddenly the story just poured out.

"It happened one morning when we were all asleep. He had a

big pain in his chest and Mom was yelling. Somehow we got in the car in our pajamas. Everything was messed up. I was in the front seat with my sister, Mary, my brother was driving, Mom and Dad were in back. Dad's head was on Mom's lap, right behind Joe, but I couldn't look. Joe was driving so fast that he slid around every corner. But inside the car was silent. Mom and us didn't say a word. It was fifty miles of no one saying anything and Joe sliding on the corners. The only sound was Dad moaning and Mary crying.

"Finally we skidded into the hospital parking lot and Joe laid on the horn. An army of nurses poured out and hauled Dad into the building. Us kids just sat outside in the cold, staring at the glass doors until Mom came back out and told Joe to take us home. Then I climbed in the backseat of that station wagon. Man, I admit it, I was so scared, just really, really scared. Nothing was ever the same after that because Dad survived that one, but not for long."

Then I shut up and looked away from the other boys, surprised at how much I'd revealed. I grabbed the cigarettes from Macek and crushed them in my hand. "No cigarettes in our hangout," I growled. "That's rule number one."

The guys sat silent for a minute, then Taylor blurted, "I gotta pee." When he came back, he said, "If this is going to be a real secret hangout, then we got to keep it a secret."

That became rule number two.

"And no one can bring anybody here without the permission of the rest of us, even girls," added Billy.

Business finished, we settled back to enjoy our getaway. Each of us had come prepared with comic books, but it was too dark to read in the smoky lean-to, so we told jokes and ghost stories. After awhile, I wondered nervously why this wasn't more fun. The location was fine, but it was just a lean-to in the woods. And there was no getting around the mosquitoes. I swatted one for effect. When rain started rattling on the metal roof, it was the last straw.

I decided right then I'd get them to move to the Caribou Club. I couldn't help think of the Caribou Club and how it might be the best hangout ever. A real place with walls and size, and it was there in the middle of all the things that weren't ours. It would be so bold to have a hangout right in plain sight.

I was glad when the others got restless too and we decided to head for Taylor's house where we crowded into the tent. Here our little quartet suffered much the same joy that we had shared in the smoky fort. I fell asleep much sooner than I ever expected, not even lasting to play strip poker, which was Macek's big plan for the evening.

I woke in the pale dusk of the Alaskan summer night. Taylor was crawling through the tent flap. He carried all the makings for peanut butter and jelly sandwiches. "Hungry?" he asked, smiling like the fox fresh from the chicken house.

Once we'd finished our too-early breakfast, Taylor made an announcement: "Gentlemen, have I got a mission for us."

"It's gotta be three in the morning, Taylor!" I growled.

"I know, and that means the time has come for action."

"Nope," I said, "I am not going until I know where and why." I was surprised at my own forcefulness.

"Okay. I know where we can get more comics, the latest, for free."

"Right."

"I swear. Cross my heart, hope to die."

Why did I believe a guy who took pride in his lies almost as much as Macek? Why did I agree to go even if it was true? Why not?

The other two took no convincing at all, so we were off, sneaking first along the alley behind Taylor's neighbors, then walking boldly, looking and listening for cars, cop cars especially. Already my heart beat too fast, and I was panting, just walking and I was panting. We didn't look at each other, so I felt alone in my tension, in my fear.

What was I doing? Mom said I was to go to Taylor's, nowhere else, not out running around the streets at three in the morning, not stealing comic books, not following a dedicated liar on some stupid adventure. My heart pounded.

I might be starting to get sick of Macek and Taylor already, but man was this exciting.

Along the main street a small shopping center had developed across from the Big G Drive-In. That was our destination. We passed the Texaco station with its giant star now dim in the predawn gray and paused behind the station dumpster, then dashed across the street. Four sweaty bodies pressed against the cinder blocks of a beauty parlor. I took inventory and concluded that Taylor was either headed for the drugstore or the grocery. Surely Taylor didn't intend to break in. Not me, no chance.

We edged around the corner and stopped cold. A police car was moving so slowly, we didn't even hear it. But there it sat like a great cat on the search for mice. The black-and-white Ford purred slowly through the parking lot of the shopping center, streaming its spotlight through the windows of the stores that formed an L around the empty rectangle of concrete.

Macek gasped and might have yelled if Taylor hadn't knocked him down as he turned to dash for cover. Billy grabbed my shoulder and spun me so fast that we both stumbled over Macek just as he bounced to his knees. Taylor waited for no one.

He dashed to the shadows and gestured desperately as we crawled, rolled, and stumbled through the alley litter to the shadows offered by the beauty parlor. As I crawled into the safety of darkness, I snuck a quick look at the police car that still idled through the parking lot.

"We're dead if he sees us!" declared Taylor. "You stupid jerks."

"We gotta run . . . for it," I said between breaths. "You're not caught until . . . you're caught." And as soon as I could inhale I was going to be running. There were enough houses, cars, bushes, and dumpsters that I knew could hide one scared kid. If I had to, I could disappear. Then I could be home in bed, safe, in fifteen minutes. This could be all over, history, if I could only breathe.

"Hang loose," ordered Billy suddenly cool. "He didn't see us."

"How do you know?" Macek said. There was surrender in his voice, panic.

"Look for yourself. He's not moving like he would if he had spotted us. Just hang loose. Be cool!"

So we hung loose. We waited for what felt like hours. And slowly, miraculously, the patrol car moved away, cruising across the lot and out onto the street.

As we let out our collective breaths, Taylor pointed to the six tidy bundles tied up with string. They lay just steps away from us. But they were out in the open and we were hugging the wall in the shadows. "Comics," Taylor whispered. We gaped at the stacks of comic books before us on the sidewalk, left there for the drugstore, for us. They lay there with the crumpled paper cups and cigarette butts outside the metal fence and heavy bars that protected the other merchandise of the store. Taylor hadn't lied.

"You mean they just drop them there?"

"Yup, the truck comes by after midnight and drops them at the door, just like your morning paper." He was obviously quite proud of himself. I wished suddenly, again, that I was home. I should have run when the cop showed up. Now I was caught with no real reason to leave and show the guys my yellow stripe. I was so unprepared, so lacking in training for such a heist. What opportunity did a homestead kid have for such larceny?

"Let's go," Billy hissed, the tension leaking out from between his teeth and through his clenched fingers. Macek was all jitters and kept dancing like he had to go. *I* sure did. In fact, I unzipped right there and let my tension splatter the already yellow wall of the beauty parlor. Of course that's when they launched the final assault. The last ounce of my urine spilled down the front of me as I turned to follow. For miles it seemed, we raced down the sidewalk past the barbershop, dry cleaners, and pet store. I was out of breath when we swept by the pool hall, then the sewing shop.

"This is too far; we'll be seen." I thought, Turn back before we're caught and me with pee running down my leg. Before I could chicken out, Taylor was there, and without breaking stride he scooped the first bundle and disappeared around the building.

I couldn't run anymore, but I did. It was like those dreams when you run from some monster but your feet go nowhere, nowhere forever, and you wake up screaming. But I couldn't wake up, and now Billy was there and he grabbed and disappeared.

I had followed Macek's chubby butt for its whole jiggling romp toward the comics, but I got there at the same time, and his panting roared louder than the echo of our Keds slapping the concrete. Two hands on one bundle. I swore and grabbed another, but before I could disappear around the corner, Taylor and Billy reappeared with panic showing through their sweat.

"Cops!!!"

Without looking to see the cop car entering the parking lot, I tucked my bundle like a football, pivoted, and dashed past the other boys in their hideaway. I wanted distance, so I ran for the sanctuary of the beauty parlor as if some magic would protect me if I returned to the wall I had marked with my pee. They joined me. Macek's bundle went up and came down like a grenade, splattering *Time* magazines all over the no-parking zone. I had to pee again.

I led the escape past the storefronts, past the echoes of our running feet, past the wall I had marked like a dog. I was drowning in sweat and about to wet my pants. Where did all that pee come from?

A row of dumpsters lined the back of the grocery store and there we hid, hovering on throbbing feet with our guts rammed up our throats so we couldn't breathe. Once more the cop car rolled slowly past us. Too slowly.

"Keep rolling, keep rolling," I whispered.

I have never been that scared before. Even on the water when the big waves were at our skiff, I hadn't been that scared. Or maybe it was guilt more than fear that was bothering me. This was supposed to be exciting and fun, but it had been neither.

The cop car kept driving and left the lot, but suddenly, I didn't want to be a thief. I didn't even like comics that much. For the first time, I actually looked at the bundle in my arms. I tore away the newsprint and cotton string. A bright picture appeared, a photograph of a delightful chocolate cake. Red print promising a recipe and diet tips inside.

Ladies' Home Journal!!

Chapter 8

The early dawn of summer had fully lighted our crime by the time we returned to the tent with one bundle of two dozen *Baby Huey* and *Richie Rich* comic books. I lay in my sleeping bag for a long time after the others fell asleep and wondered what was so cool about going out and getting the piss scared out of me. What a waste of a good night's sleep.

A siren woke me in a panic, but I finally realized it was just Taylor's mom calling us from the back door. "Andy! Andy Taylor!" she called with a shrill demanding hail. "You boys can't sleep all day!" The sun was like the policeman's spotlight when Billy pulled back the tent flap and I shrank from my guilt. Everyone else seemed to act innocent and this helped me survive the naked sensation of walking in the open across the sunlit lawn in the same shoes, clothes, and face I had worn during the big comic book heist. All three of my accomplices were calm and relaxed. Not me. Every neighbor must be looking; every car that passed must see that these were the ones, those four boys who stole the comics and even those ladies' magazines too!

Taylor's mom made us sandwiches and hovered over the table like a helicopter. No one looked at her face, and we were afraid to look at each other, except Taylor, of course, who kept a steady banter going, as if we really were just four normal kids, not wanted criminals.

Mrs. Taylor smiled sweet as grape jam and asked, "So, Samuel, what does your father do?"

At that moment I had just taken a bite of a Miracle Whip, bologna, and Wonder Bread sandwich when some special physics occurred when I tried to speak. As soon as I opened my mouth, everything stuck right to my palate. I could not even mumble something as simple as "Uh-huh." Words wouldn't even form and my tongue got in the way, so I ended up looking like I was having a spaz attack.

I tried to swallow, deep and purposefully. Then, knowing better as I did it, I drank, forcing the Kool-Aid in between my crowded tongue and the swelling log of sandwich. The Kool-Aid was like glue that permanently attached the massive wad of sandwich. Something like Jell-O ran out both sides of my mouth as I gasped for air.

Wiping my chin on my sleeve, I was actually thankful for the extra seconds to think. What should I say to Mrs. Taylor? No grown-up had asked me that since things had gone crazy back in March. In fact, I had never met anyone before who didn't already know my parents and my whole life story.

Mrs. Taylor handed Taylor another sandwich and took my silence as an invitation to ask another question. "Is your father stationed here at the air force base?"

My face turned red. I could feel it. And my eyes watered.

I shook my head, and, suddenly, the mass on my palate dislodged, I gulped it down, and blurted out, "He's dead."

Poor Mrs. Taylor, blasted with a missile, went gray and wiped her face on her apron. Taylor turned to stare, his cheeks full of bologna while Macek nearly choked on a cookie.

"Oh, Sam, I am so sorry. I had no idea."

She was sorry? I was the one who should be sorry. She hadn't asked to get hit like that when she wasn't looking. If she were a kid it would be different. Kids don't look that far ahead that something like that would set them back, but for a polite grown-up like Mrs. Taylor it was a punch in the gut.

"It's okay, really," I said. And it was. It was the way things were. Dad was dead and the only time it was hard for me was when Mom got blue, or at times like this.

Mrs. Taylor collected herself and got nosy. "How long has your father been . . . gone?"

"He died last fall. It was a heart attack," I said, before she had time to ask.

"Oh, your poor mother."

I grabbed another sandwich and hoped she'd quit asking questions. I didn't mind thinking about my dad, in fact, I enjoyed it; I just didn't like sharing it with strangers.

Taylor broke the spell. "Hey, you wanna ride bikes or something? We could play *Combat* in the lot."

"Yeah, *Combat*!" I nearly cheered. I had no idea what *Combat* was, but I was thrilled to leave the questions behind.

The lot was the vacant one where the Quonset hut sat surrounded by a litter of bottles, boxes, sticks, and old fence pieces. The grass was high and unkempt, zigzagged with bike paths and dog trails. No one mentioned the heist or the comics we got from it.

"I'm Sarge," Taylor said, "Macek, you're Little John. Billy, you're Doc. Sam, you can be Kirby."

"Who's Kirby?" I hadn't meant to blow my cover; it just came out. The game stopped for a moment.

"Who's Kirby? Where you been living, under a rock?" sneered Macek.

"I . . . I've never seen *Combat*," I stuttered. "We didn't have TV in Ninilchik. Still don't."

The mouths that dropped open in disbelief told me that I had gained, not lost, and they admired me with the sympathy and awe reserved only for those who have been released from a Russian salt mine.

"No TV? Your mom should be arrested!" cried Taylor.

They proceeded to tell me all about the World War II TV show about a platoon of soldiers fighting their way across France. They let me pick my character. Kirby sounded fine.

Taylor and I were intensely stalking an imaginary German soldier who had disappeared behind a bundle of fencing when a gaggle of girls wandered into our view. Our machine guns fell silent as lonely soldiers stared from beneath their helmets. The girls walked on, ignoring our haggard faces in the weeds. Seeing them made me feel silly playing a kids' game in the grass, and I wanted instead to follow them.

"Red fox leader," Macek called from his hiding place. "This is Sergeant Sanders. We have orders to follow those spies and find their hideout." As if their mystery required any enhancement, the girls immediately became SS agents. We became their shadows.

Keeping to the dusty potholed alleys, we followed the targets as they roamed into the neighborhood on the bluff above C Street. Our interest ran out when the girls failed to notice us, so we gave up our prey for another raid on the Taylorses' fridge and huddled on the steps munching cold wieners.

"Carpenter's dreams!" cried Macek, waving a limp wiener down the street toward the girls. "Flat as boards!" He laughed, but only Taylor joined him. I was getting sick of Macek's mouth.

Taylor was staring at the steps between his knees. "Why did you do that, Sam?"

"Do what?"

"You know, how could you say that about your dad? To my mom."

"But he *is* dead."

"Yeah, but you didn't need to say it that way."

"What was I *supposed* to say?"

"All those fancy words like 'passed away', or 'no longer with us'?"

"Leave him alone, Taylor," said Billy. There was fresh challenge in his voice, and I admired him. "I'm going home," he said. But he didn't leave until he went to the tent and grabbed a pile of the comics, stuffing them in his pack with his sleeping bag.

I grew sullen and silent. What did Taylor know about people dying? Who made that stupid bigmouth an expert on post-funeral etiquette?

I wanted to tell him so, about how it wasn't easy to say those words no matter what they were and that it was me who deserved sympathy, not other people with hurt feelings. I could have told him that nosy people like his mom got what they deserved. But I didn't. Sometimes I'm not good at saying what needs to be said, and I guess that's what the argument was about anyway.

Not one damn bit of it made my dad less dead or our home in Ninilchik any closer. I found an excuse to go home and scuffed along the dusty alleyways, feeling sorry for myself and reviewing the wasted fantasies I had concocted about Anchorage and life in the big city.

I imagined being on a shiny bike cruising along the pavement, leading a pack of admiring friends to a baseball game on a real diamond with grass and bases. Then it was a trip to the movies with mountains of popcorn and laughs and hamburgers and shakes every day. We lived on a street with sidewalks and gutters in a neighborhood with picket fences, lawns stocked with croquet sets, second-story windows, and television. The guy next door was my best friend, but not as tall or fast as I was, and his mom made the best cookies in the world.

Back home, I would have been miles from the tiny village we called a town, a homestead slave for the summer, chained to a hoe and a shovel. Maybe fishing with Dad had just been one of my silly dreams too. In the big city now, fourteen and pretty much on my own, this was supposed to be the summer of all summers, but here I was walking a dusty gravel street alone with my neck full of mosquito bites and two jerks for friends.

Even though I sometimes felt like a prisoner there, I longed for my old Ninilchik place on the bluff where the clothes flapped on the line, and my sister and I fought as we pulled weeds in the garden, and there were no comic books to steal. The vegetables would all be planted now, and maybe I'd wander out to the tree house and put the roof on it. With the sun shining and the chores done, I might find that soft hollow in the woods along the clearing edge and dream up a tale with me as the hero.

By the time I reached my street and crossed the gravel parking lot with its potholes still full of old rain, I had transported myself so far that I didn't notice the smell of mold and dank laundry when I clomped up the front steps of the green apartment building and into the musty stairwell that led to our two-bedroom apartment on the second floor.

Chapter 9

One Sunday I leaned out the window and saw Joe getting out of a brand-new 1965 Mustang.

"Wow! Neat car!" I yelled. It seemed to hug the pavement, poised for one command from whoever held the keys, the keys my brother jangled before me. Joe had a new apartment and new friends, but most Sundays he came to do his weekly chore: be a son and big brother.

"Where did you get the money for *that?*" asked Mom, suspicion dripping from her mouth. She leaned on her kitchen mop and wiped her face with a dish towel.

Joe stepped forward bravely. "Credit, Mom, credit. I couldn't believe it. I haven't been working that long and they still gave me credit. Come on. Take a look."

"Can you afford it?"

"Sure, I'm making good money."

"Your father never bought a car on credit."

Joe cowered. I was discovering that evoking the dead is as

powerful as a witch's curse. He chatted around it as he showed us his new toy. With my face pressed against the glass, I stared at the evidence that Joe had reached a point that was so far out in front of me that it seemed forever out of reach. I could remember when we built our tree fort and stole canned peaches from the pantry to eat there together. Now we were beyond that and so far apart it was as if somewhere along the way he had rushed ahead while I stood still.

The bright new car was glaring evidence that Joe was no kid anymore, forever. Mom could argue and cajole and whine, but he could walk out and drive away. Like a cowboy's horse, a car set a man free, free and apart from a kid who didn't even own a bicycle.

That day we were so amazed to be riding in this new fast car that Mary and I didn't even fight. I just lay against the vinyl seats and drew in that sweet new car smell. The aroma carried me off into a fantasy with me behind the wheel of my own car, cruising the endless highway of the American West, a highway that flowed over the desert like a black ribbon of freedom. Along that highway were only gas stations and drive-in hamburger joints with trays to hang on your window so you never had to leave the saddle. The hot wind of the desert folded back my hair and there was nothing but the throb of the car engine.

This ride was so different from the last trip with Joe when we drove Dad to the hospital. Joe was driving fast again, but this time for fun. We were out on the Glenn Highway thundering along toward the mountains and away from the city. Each time we passed a car he downshifted and the force of acceleration threw us back in our seats. He wanted us to feel the power, to experience how totally he could reach beyond what tethered us to him. And I could—I could feel him disappearing from us, like Dad had.

Mom just said, "Joe, slow down and quit showing off." He

drove home obediently and let us off at the curb without coming in to eat. He just rumbled away with all the people staring at him from the sidewalk.

That afternoon Mom must have felt my misery for she took me to a secondhand store to find a bike. The shop was located between a pawnshop and a laundromat. There were bars on the windows and broken washers and lawn mowers out front.

"So you want a bike, huh?" The owner was a fat and buck-toothed man with his lunch on his shirt. "Come on out back, kid." He patted me on the shoulder, and I didn't want to go anywhere with him. Mom pushed me along, and we followed the shuffling form past mounds of musty books and old clothes, past a mountain of mildewed army uniforms and through a rattling steel door.

Only one bike had both wheels on it and he pulled it proudly from its rest against the building wall. The bike was big, full-sized with fat tires, like tractor tires. The fenders were gone, fleeing perhaps in shame. And worst of all, the bicycle worked. I'd have to say yes. I'd have to tell Mom that this was great.

When I returned from my test ride around the tiny parking lot, Mom was closing her purse and the man had a ten in his fat fingers, and he handed me a new seat that was part of the deal.

What I wanted to say, but didn't was, Thank you for a bike right out of ancient times. Thank you for getting me the biggest bike on Government Hill, maybe in the whole state. Thank you for not letting me pick out a new bike with high handlebars and a banana seat.

Instead, what I said was, "Thanks, Mom. This is great!"

I had been pleading for a bike since we got to Anchorage: "It doesn't matter what it looks like, and it don't have to be new," I said. "I just want a bike; something to ride around on and go to the store and stuff." Stuff meant freedom, mobility, personal transportation, something to hold me over until I could buy a car and have some real wheels. I got what I asked for and no more.

Mary was full of encouragement. There was never halfway with Mary; she either liked something or hated it. She was on the liking side that day, so she pranced and pointed, oohing and ahh-ing, until I was thoroughly disgusted. She was trying to cheer me up, but I just pedaled off to mope. It was a Sunday afternoon with the emptiness that felt lonely and made me remember Sunday picnics and Dad napping in the sun.

I rode up and down the whole of Government Hill, one minute glad to be mobile and free, the next morose and disappointed with the bike that was no better than the one I left in Ninilchik. I circled the Caribou Club and thought about going in, but stopped at the Big G instead. I didn't have the money for grilled and greasy, so I went for sugar.

A pretty waitress leaned over the counter and asked, "What would you like?" She was a blond teenager with bright eyes, and her closeness embarrassed me. I don't think she knew because she smiled so gently that I felt somehow that she would never purpose-fully embarrass even a younger kid like me who would be honored just to share the same air she breathed.

"Root beer and a pineapple sundae," I answered.

She set a water glass before me and I watched helplessly as her fingers unwrapped from it. Instantly, I forgot Becky and all the starlets in every movie I'd ever seen.

I had only started noticing girls' bodies a few months ago, but hers seemed to be shaped more perfectly than any. The waitress uniform fit her like an evening gown and her legs reached down from the short hem like sculptured ivory. I stared at the hands that poured the root beer and shoulders that tensed as she dug out the ice cream from the big tubs. Her bottom showed round against the skirt as she arched upward to reach the pineapple topping.

"Do you always have that?" she asked placing the root beer and sundae before me.

"Yup, always." I wished I'd had a Big G sundae before so I'd know if she'd given me extra.

"Doesn't that give you a headache? Ice cream and soda together?" What was this? She was having a conversation with me. The queen speaking to the pauper. I studied her mouth as she made words. I glanced at her eyes that promised never to be cruel.

A man came to the walkup window, and I wanted to kill him for interrupting us, but then I thanked him for letting me see her move. A ballerina in tennis shoes making milkshakes, her blond ponytail bouncing in counter-rhythm with her hips. And she didn't ask the person at the window if that was always what they ordered.

When she came back along the counter I read her name tag: Shirley.

Like a novice swimmer I tested new water. "Shirley," I said, tasting the magic of the name, "can I have another glass of water?"

"Yes, sir, coming right up," she answered with a grin.

I owned the sky!

"My, you do eat slowly," she said when she brought me another glass of water. I nodded and regretfully swallowed the last bit of ice cream. I left a little in the bottom of my root beer glass, so that I wouldn't make disgusting gurgling noises with the straw.

Shirley was, I decided, an even better heroine for my fantasies than Vivien Leigh, the movie star. Now she was gone, forgotten like an old shoe. I walked out of the Big G heedless of little else but Shirley. Becky was history. No other woman had ever lived who could compare. The rusty out-of-date bike was forgotten, and I rode home on a cloud of wonder.

I was still in a great mood even two days later when I saw my friends for the first time since the comic book caper. They were sitting on the curb beside the Texaco station sucking exhaust as they ogled the passing cars. Nothing quite excited our minds like the raucous power of the internal combustion engine. Even a lawn mower could, for a half hour at least, be more exciting and inspiring than a girl in cutoff jeans. From where we sat, the only difference between us and high schoolers was a foot in height and a car.

Girls gave us a deep painful yearning, but cars we worshipped just as we were taught. Cars were something that I knew more about than the others. Dad and Joe had spent many hours in the shop with their heads under the hood of the station wagon. In the temple of our shop, the sacred ritual of the overhaul and rebuild had taken place many times: a ceremony with oil, grease, and four-letter words.

The vehicle fascination began early for boys in our family first with tricycles, then bikes, but those were only toys. Put an engine on those wheels, rev it up and go. Before long, my brother and I learned the litany of the carburetor, four-speed transmissions, rods and pistons.

Here in Anchorage it wasn't much different, except boys hung out at the Texaco station, watching men wipe the sacred grease off their hands, pump gas, stick their noses under hoods of mystery.

A Buick sedan roared by, trailing a cloud of blue smoke. "That sucker needs a new set of rings," I observed wisely that day as we sat on the curb car watching.

Taylor wanted to be expert at everything. "Could be failed plugs," he said.

"Nope. Blue smoke means the damn thing's burning oil. Nothing but a set of rings will fix that." I was using my father's words, keeping him alive with the little pieces that I had saved.

"Pardon me, Mr. Pro Mechanic," pouted Taylor.

"Wouldn't fix a piece of junk like that anyway," insisted Macek. "You won't find me driving a clunker like that."

We watched the cars passing us along the streets in a parade of chrome and thunder, washing us with the ambrosia of their hot exhaust. The cars passed heedless of the boys perched on the curb, and we soon moved on to other distractions.

"My dad always drove Fords," I volunteered.

"Not me," said Macek. "Gotta have a Chrysler for the chrome and the big fins."

"I ain't never gonna own a car," said Taylor. "It's gonna be a truck. A big dually truck."

Suddenly Billy stood up and pointed. All he said was, "Wow!" We followed him as he walked along the hill over Bluff Road following a dark spaceship of a car as it slowly passed out of our view in the traffic of downtown.

Macek looked at Billy and said, "What was that? I never!"

"That was a brand-new Corvette Stingray fastback," I said. We all held a moment of silence to savor what we had seen. It was only the second one I'd ever seen in real life, much more exciting than my model. Then Taylor broke the moment and pitched a dirt clod at a particularly ugly station wagon passing by. We watched as it arced and fell short at the edge of the road.

"Nice throw, Bozo!" Macek jeered.

"If I had a water balloon you'd have seen something," he answered.

"Water balloons!!" four voices yelled at once.

In half an hour we were back with a jug of water and a stash of balloons, flat and innocent in their happy birthday package. We nearly trembled with excitement as we filled them and stacked jiggling piles that looked like Easter eggs made of Jell-O. Even though the thick brush and trees along the hill above the road hid us from view, I wasn't feeling too good about this.

"I don't know guys. This could go really wrong," Billy said, voicing my fears.

But the others ignored him. "Hey, big boys!" Taylor called in a high voice. He held two bulging balloons to his chest and did a little dance that made them jiggle.

"Gross!" I yelled and grabbed one of his falsies. The balloon exploded and showered both of us with water.

"Okay, you jerk. That does it!" Taylor pitched his remaining balloon at me, but missed by a mile.

"Don't waste ammo," Billy ordered. "It's D-Day!" He pointed down the hill to the lines of cars.

Taylor, seemingly devoid of fear, broke our deadlock by rushing to the edge of the bluff and hurling his water grenades in one swift volley. I watched them go end over end, changing shape as they went. Four necks stretched out to follow their path. One seemed headed for a sedan but dropped harmlessly to the asphalt. The second shattered atop a bread truck.

"Kaboom!" we shouted.

Macek rushed forward to unload a big blue balloon at a gray Corvette that had just rolled into view. Billy threw him to the ground with a big shove to the back. The balloon broke on the ground and Macek got up cursing.

"Don't hit the 'Vettes, man!" Billy screamed, then more calmly, "we don't bomb the 'Vettes." I looked at him closely.

He wasn't nuts, he just carried his passion all the way through.

"Have a cow while you're at it," chided Taylor.

"I mean it guys," Billy was almost in tears. "They're just too cool."

"Okay," I volunteered, "Corvettes are on our side." And I was pretty confident that we wouldn't see another one in the same afternoon.

Everyone took turns with the wet grenades. Three stood audience and critiqued the thrower, stretching the thrill of our recklessness. Colored balls of water sailed harmlessly into the brush or along the asphalt. Only a couple of motorists even noticed that they were under attack, but they just yelled at us and kept driving.

I waited my turn, holding back and licking my mouth, which was suddenly dry. Then I rushed to the very edge of the bluff and with a bold yell heaved one and then another red water balloon into the void.

My throws were hard and fast, and as the last left my hand I remembered being seven, and Ben Flowers and me in the bushes along the Sterling Highway. There was a car then too, and Ben's rock hit the glass. We were running with a voice screaming at us to stop. I remember Dad spanking me, the flat of his hand on my tiny behind. We weren't bad; the car had just appeared. Though I wondered now if Ben had really seen the car and had tried to hit it, just as I was trying to now.

As soon as they left, I wanted those balloons to return to my hands, looping back like boomerangs, but they continued to soar out and away. The first hit a power pole with a splat that seemed to echo across the city, and the other went on. I didn't breathe. A sedan with the windows rolled down came into view with a windshield jutting up as big as a movie screen. Surely the balloon wouldn't hit the windshield. It couldn't.

But it did. Like a guided missile it swept over the reaching alders and struck the windshield full in the face of the driver.

How is it that time can freeze in one explosive moment, hanging like a parachute that will not fall? In the same moment, events rush past in a desperate flurry. A collage of blond hair, blue fenders, sunglasses, and a shattered red balloon filled my vision.

"Bull's eye!" Taylor cheered, drowning out my gasp. Billy and Macek rushed forward to get a better view.

Below, the Chrysler swerved to the right and bumped up over the curb and out of my view. I craned my neck but couldn't see past the thick foliage. But I could certainly hear the squealing brakes and blaring horns. Shouts wafted out of open car windows. Then a Chevy wagon practically stood on its nose as it skidded to a stop. My heart skidded to a stop as well.

"Run!" screamed a voice that sounded like mine. Billy grabbed my arm and pulled.

Accusing faces looked up from car windows into the alders. I fled with the others, unused water balloons tumbling into the weeds and splattering on the ground around our running sneakers.

It was only one hundred yards through the woods to a gravel street where we stumbled into the open, feeling naked and scared as rabbits in a dog pound. The heavy breathing and tightness in my chest were not from the short dash. Guilt was hitting me like an attack of malaria, hurting my gut and stretching my skin like I had too much blood. I rubbed the back of my aching neck with a cold hand and looked at my accomplices.

They too looked at the ground, not at me, or each other, choking on the fear and guilt that made us suddenly strangers. Taylor stood with what looked like wide-eyed excitement and near joy. I could see that he alone was enjoying this moment. Then we continued our escape, through the back alleys and vacant lots to the side of the hill where the path cut through the fireweed and down a steep gully to our hangout.

Macek broke the silence with a gasp. "Fingerprints!" he whispered. "They can get our fingerprints off the water jugs . . . and the balloons."

Taylor laughed, "You stupid wimp. They have to match fingerprints. Unless you've been arrested nobody has your fingerprints."

"Haven't you?" Macek asked.

"Up yours, moron," Taylor said. He jumped the smaller boy and started a one-sided wrestling match that ended with a noogie on Macek's head.

Suddenly, feeling tired and alone, I rose and started up the trail. "I'm going home. See ya later, guys." I felt their eyes scratching my back as I waded through the grass that I wished would swallow me whole. The distant sirens multiplied in my panicked imagination. I pictured hundreds of cops following packs of drooling hounds along the secret path to our fort and my front door.

The rest of the day I rolled around on my bed. I couldn't turn off the movie that ran over and over in my brain. The oblong balloon lofting over the alders and smashing onto the windshield of the Chrysler, exploding water, the screech of brakes. It was nothing at all like I imagined. I had pictured soft water balloons tumbling out of the air and dropping in front of cars or plopping on their hoods with a splash and a laugh.

But instead I had this. I was feeling sick and couldn't sleep thinking maybe that guy in the Chrysler was hurt. I buried my face

in my pillow. Taylor didn't care. I'd heard him laughing as we ran. Macek and Billy, home safe, were probably laughing too. Why couldn't I laugh about it? I hated my stupid fear, and guilt, and my pessimism that couldn't conceive of anything but the worst for Sam Barger.

Chapter 16

The story was in the paper the next morning but the cops never came to my door. A photo of the angry driver standing next to his car, parked up on the sidewalk half in the weeds. The article made it sound like the water balloon was a bazooka shell. I was relieved to read that the car hadn't actually crashed, but only swerved up on the sidewalk and bounced into the weeds without hurting anybody. Taylor cut the article out and put it on the wall above his bed and would have kept talking about it for a month if it hadn't been for the Caribou Club and one burgundy Corvette.

Once I realized that the police would not track me down and arrest me for throwing a water balloon, I rekindled my resolve to take the Caribou Club. We were finishing a yard job for Billy's next-door neighbor when Macek and Taylor came by and wanted to go back to the gully.

"Forget the gully," I said, "forget we ever even saw it. We have a hangout to beat all hangouts." Billy gave me a glance, as if to say, "Are you sure about this?" But I was sure and continued, "This is the Corvette Stingray of hideouts. And it's right here in your own neighborhood." I started laughing at myself for sounding like a used car salesman on TV.

"Are you wacko?" asked Macek. "There ain't no such thing around here unless you're talking about the Quonset hut."

Taylor jumped in, "Not the hut. I hate that place. Too many older guys using it at night and everybody knows about it. Let's go to the gully. It's not raining today so it'll be great."

"Great if you like mosquitoes biting your butt. Great if dark and wet is your idea of comfortable. Tell 'em, Billy. Tell 'em how great our spot is!"

Billy laughed and jumped over the fence to join us in the alley behind his house. "It is far-out, guys. Far-out!"

"The gully's just some stupid boards and a bunch of plastic," I insisted.

"Stupid! But we worked a whole day on the gully," whined Macek.

"But your dumb spot is better?" Taylor asked.

"Yup," Billy added.

"Doesn't even compare!" I said with a grin. It was a relief to finally tell them about it. Now we just had to convince them to check it out. "Really. Come on, we'll show you. What could be cooler than having a hangout right in plain sight?"

Taylor stared at the ground. "I can't go right now. I've got stuff to do."

"Since when?" asked Billy. "Come on, Taylor. Let's go."

He shook his head. Suddenly I understood. Taylor always picked our games and pranks. The Caribou Club was new and big and he wanted it to be *his* idea.

"We need you guys," I offered. "You're good at figuring

things out and making stuff better." The plan unfolded for me as I continued talking. "With the four of us, we can clean up the club and make it really cool. You'll see, it's something special!"

Finally, Taylor gave in, but as we walked to the Caribou Club he remained unconvinced that Billy and I could find a place, a wonderful place right there in his own neighborhood, a neighborhood where he roamed free stealing comics with impunity.

When we finally escorted him into the Caribou Club and he saw the main room bathed in the glow of our flashlights, when we marched through the rattle of paper into the main hall, his total silence told me he approved.

Billy, who had been quiet during the walk over, rushed to the bandstand where he danced in our tiny spotlights and sang the latest Beatles song. He strummed a ghost guitar and made us laugh. The laughter echoed in the hall.

"You wanna hold my hand?" giggled Macek. "What a queer!"

"You oughta know!" I answered.

"Huh?"

Billy and I rushed him together and pitched him to the floor. "Taylor!" he yelped. But Taylor was already off exploring. I snatched Macek's light and we left him in the middle of the floor. Switching our lights off we dove behind the curtain and waited in the stillness.

"Real funny, guys."

Silence. Darkness.

"Billy. Sam. Taylor! Where are you guys? Knock it off! Billl-lyy!" The darkness in the hall was complete and Macek was alone in it.

We pinched our noses and waited in silence, then we rustled the heavy curtains and moaned deep and sinister. We could hear

Macek's breathing coming hard and tight. "Taylor, you better get out here right this goddamned minute!" Macek was begging now.

Then the curtains moved, first furtively, and then without a sound, we were sprayed with a barrage of light. Red, green, yellow, and white spotlights scorched our dilated pupils and froze us mid-step. Momentarily our hearts and minds rushed away from us out the back door, across the parking lot, and into the arms of our parents.

"Shiiittt!" yelled Billy.

"AAAhhh!!" I screamed.

And from the hall before us, Macek yelled, "Ooohh Gaawd!"

"Ta da!" cheered Taylor as he leaped from behind the curtains and into the glare of the lights.

"Where'd the lights come from?" I asked.

"There's a switch, stupid." He held a broom handle like a microphone and tried to talk but laughter and total self-satisfaction had overtaken him and he writhed hysterically. "You guys . . . you . . . were . . . so damn . . . funny."

"Taylor, you jerk!" I laughed.

Then he found a modicum of control. "Yes, folks, we have a reaallly bbiigg shew tonight."

Billy was calm. "Is that your best Ed Sullivan impression?"

"Not bad, huh?" Taylor still struggled with fits of laughter. "Oh, I loved it. You twerps thought it was all over."

"No, we didn't," I lied for the three of us.

In the center of the dance hall, Macek hunkered as if he had melted into a little pile of bird poop. He didn't look at us or at anything, he was just heaped there amid the paper, and he shuddered a little.

"Macek? Macek?" I called. "Are you okay?"

He leaped suddenly to his feet. "No, I'm not! Taylor, all you guys, if you ever do anything like that again I'll kick your ass. You stupid jerk morons."

Taylor laughed. "Are you mad, Macek?" he asked, leaning over with his hands on his knees.

"Up your nose, Andrew Taylor, you son-of-a-bitch."

"My mother wasn't a dog. You've met her."

We laughed and Macek almost did. He crept to the elevated bandstand and joined us in the footlights.

"Bet she spits rice when you kiss her," he said softly, finally scoring.

This time Taylor didn't laugh, but it didn't stop the rest of us. And it didn't stop the moron jokes that followed there in the lights of the stage where we were the stars and the audience for the only people that really mattered. Taylor got to finish playing Ed Sullivan and then we were all the Beatles and standup comics.

I used my fingers to mash my face around. "Watch this guys," I said and turned my eyelids inside out.

"Sick!"

"First time I saw that, I was too small to laugh so I just rolled over and shit."

"Yeah, then your mom threw away the wrong pile."

We joked and played and explored through the afternoon, taking possession just by being there. It was a stolen time in an off-limits place. We could have been on the moon, we were so separated from the world. Dancing, cursing, singing, forgetting all the rules that our parents taught us. It was like we found a place behind the sign that said, "No Trespassing, Adults Only."

I left the dirty old building feeling tired and thirsty. The afternoon in the Caribou Club had been a parching experience.

With a quarter in my pocket and the Big G on the way home, not to mention the chance of seeing Shirley, my mouth was as dry as the desert in a Borax soap commercial.

"Hi!" I called when I saw her.

"Well, hello stranger. The usual?" she answered with a smile.

Stranger—it sounded so familiar. How much more familiar could she get? She would have to jump across the counter and kiss me. Was she more wonderful than before? Could I even speak?

She left a fellow she was talking to at one of the booths and came around the counter to face me.

"I'll have a root beer, please," I managed.

"Drinking it straight today, huh?"

"Uh . . . um. . . . Ice would be okay."

She laughed, like a thousand tiny bells, like that jingling that Tinker Bell makes with her wand at the beginning of a Disney movie. I reached for the glass of water and stared in horror. My hands! I drew them back and tried to look nonchalant as I strolled to the restroom. My hands had collected the dust and grime from everything I touched that day. I scrubbed vigorously, then seeing my face in the mirror, I scrubbed it too. Even my arms took a lather and showed lighter skin beneath.

When I returned to my stool, my root beer was waiting and Shirley was giggling with the guy in the booth again. I felt small and jealous. She didn't circle back to the counter until he left, but when she did she saw my wounded arm, now bearing a massive scab from the bicycle crash.

"What happened?" she asked, touching the egg-shaped scab just below my elbow and wrinkling her perfect eyebrows in sympathy. "That must hurt."

"Nah, it's just a little scrape from a bike wreck."

"Ouch." She cared. She touched me. She *cared*. I wanted to run out and let a truck run over me so that she would spend forever tending my wounds. I watched for a half hour while she floated around the diner feeding the hungry. I fed on her motion.

I was sucking the last drops of root beer from the ice cubes in my glass when the door swung open almost voluntarily. A tall teenager in a letter jacket sauntered through. He was lean and athletic with a clean white T-shirt and creased blue jeans. He had a jaw like a cowboy hero and the rest was shoulders and teeth. Mr. Perfect leaned on the counter and said to Shirley, "Hey, how's my girl today?"

She lit up like a kitchen match. With the turn of her head toward him she slit my throat, and I bled slowly into the straw that hung stupidly out of my mouth. I saw then, for the first time, the smitten starburst of love like in the movies, and I knew more than I wanted to know.

"Hi, Allen," she chirped. Like the pineapple topping on a sundae, the words were clumpy and sweet and made my stomach hurt. I finished my root beer and slid invisibly off my stool and across a pool of my pain to the door. It squealed when I opened it, and it felt so heavy. Mr. Perfect looked up. "So long, come back and see us sometime."

Outside, the sky opened and a heavy shower poured rain in my eyes, but I couldn't leave just yet. I had to watch her and wish myself in his place. I half-heartedly admired a bright green '56 Chevy sitting alone in the lot. Small fins lifted off the rear fenders, and chrome accented the windows and headlights. The seats were shiny red and white, and all of it spotless. Clouds moved lower and darkened the sky and the rain rattled on the hood of the car. I peeked back through the shadowed window one last time and saw Shirley lean over the counter and touch her puckered lips to Mr. Perfect's cheek. I turned away, ashamed, and slunk down the sidewalk toward home, picking at the scab on my arm.

When I had covered only half a block and was pretty well soaked, a car pulled up to the curb and a window rolled down. "How about a lift?" The '56 Chevy idled at the curb with Mr. Perfect behind the wheel.

I stood there looking at the face that was talking to me, the face Shirley had kissed, and I wanted to smash it for being so cocky, handsome, and got-it-all-together-and-I'm-wearing-my-letter-jacket perfect. I had worked hard on this dream and he didn't fit in. I wasn't prepared to justify him to the illogical optimism of my fantasies.

"Hop in. You're getting soaked."

"Okay." Okay, but I won't be nice. Okay, but don't think this makes it better. Okay, but drop dead. I got in. "Nice car."

"Thanks. I just got it running. My dad and I've been working on it for two years." He smiled that I'm-a-nice-guy-big-brother-type smile and I felt better even though I didn't want to. Maybe he wasn't bragging about having a dad, maybe it just came out that way. "Where you headed?"

"My dad's dead." Once again, I blurted it out before I could even think it was a bad idea. I hastily added, "I mean, the Hollywood Arms. I'm headed there."

He extended a hand. "Allen Hanson."

I shook his hand. "Sam, Sam Barger."

"That's tough. About your dad, I mean." He was embarrassed, but so was I, so I tried to change the subject.

"My brother has a Mustang."

"Really? Those are so bad. Is it a fastback?"

"Yeah. Red and fast."

"I bet."

Silence. I looked out the window and into the vision of three girls in cutoffs pausing in the rain to wave and smile. I waved back, a short, loose-wristed, high schooler kind of wave. I wanted to keep driving forever, to cruise all of Anchorage in that '56 Chevy with Mr. Perfect, but in what felt like seconds he stopped the car and I was home.

I hopped out and reached through the window to shake hands. "Thanks for the ride. You've got a real nice girlfriend." He smiled and drove away.

On the steps I met the girl with the belly button forehead, and I asked her name. "Melissa," she answered, and I gave her a piece of gum. I wondered if she was always there sitting on the cold, indifferent concrete of the front steps, and I imagined her riding in a nice car with a boy who wanted to kiss her, but the fantasy wouldn't hold.

Chapter 11

For more than a week, the Caribou Club was the center of our waking energy and the setting for the most magnificent of dreams. If we weren't mowing lawns for spending money or riding bikes, we were hanging out at the club. I had no other distraction now that my fantasies about Shirley had been crushed by the high school letterman. Last year, Allen would have been my idol, a guy you wanted to be seen standing by at the basketball game or sitting next to on the school bus, but now he was an impossible model of reality in a time when dreams were all that you could depend on.

In the Caribou Club, none of that mattered. When Taylor discovered the spotlights, we knew we had not only space, but power, real power. Electricity. Buildings needed power all year to prevent freezing pipes. But we figured it was justified good fortune for us.

The fuses were gone from all but a couple of the spaces in the big electrical box but we found that the ones from my apartment building fit just fine. We soon had lights in the dance hall, but mostly we used the stage lights, leaving the rest of the building dark and mysterious. Even in daylight we couldn't give anyone a clue about us being in the building. This was a big secret to keep.

We brought in a radio for music and crackers and peanut butter for snacks. We had a stash of comics and *MAD* magazines in a cardboard box, so we spent some of our time just lounging around in the semidarkness rereading our favorites and telling jokes.

But it wasn't all play. I was bent on cleaning the place up, and even found a broom. I had just started sweeping up when I heard a *pop, pop, pop* exploding from the kitchen. Macek came running out with Taylor in chase. He had discovered a batch of lightbulbs and was using them like grenades to torture Macek. *Pop.* He threw another one right at Macek's feet, making him jump as he sprinted through the room.

"Knock it off!" I yelled.

"Why should I?" Taylor yelled back, still throwing bulbs. "It's fun."

"Stop breaking stuff!" hollered Billy, taking my side. "You're making a huge mess, man. You gonna clean it up?"

Taylor stopped with the bulb grenades, but things were dark and quiet for a while when he was mad at me.

Billy and I swept up all the glass scattered around the floor. We worked as we never would have at home, sweeping up garbage, bringing out some stray furniture and putting some away, generally setting things right. We found a closet by the back door where we heaped all the mostly paper trash, filling the room waist high with litter.

"What is all this paper?" Macek asked. He picked up some of the white sheets we'd been scooping.

Billy grabbed one. "Blank restaurant receipts. Must be mil-lions of them."

"Wonder who threw them all over?" Macek asked.

"Don't look at me!" growled Taylor.

"The ghost of the Caribou Club!" I announced. "Place like this must have a ghost."

Billy grinned wickedly. "Now that would so boss."

We filled the closet with the receipts, closed the door, and forgot about them, but we didn't forget about the ghost idea; hop-ing to find one, praying we didn't.

Food and drinks we kept stashed behind the counter of the restaurant where we took turns serving with flamboyant style and inflated prices that we didn't have to pay. We were in the midst of one such banquet of Kool-Aid and Oreos when Billy, waiter for the day, froze and his eyes grew wide.

"SSHH. A car," he whispered calmly.

Then we all heard it. The crunch of tires on gravel. The engine sound was muffled, but the tires crumbled across the gravel with such clarity that one could imagine each stone grinding against its neighbor to send us a warning.

"Oh no," whispered Macek, his face a pale mask in the dim light, "cops."

"Hush," I heard myself saying, as if the sound of rolling tires would tell me all I needed to know.

"Kill the lights," ordered Billy, thinking while the rest of us did nothing.

Taylor rushed to the switch. We huddled together behind the counter like a litter of deserted pups. When the tire sounds stopped we heard only the faint hum of a car's engine through the wall. We breathed only because we couldn't not. Billy munched a last Oreo and grinned bravely. He made me want to laugh. Or pee. I looked away and grabbed my nose.

Taylor caught the fever and started making faces at Billy. Trapped between them, I buried my face in my hands, imagining the wall suddenly dissolving and leaving us huddled, giggling, and naked in the spotlight of a squad car.

When the rubber crushed gravel again, we could hear it moving away from our hiding place. Taylor rushed to a window that had a peephole through the boards. "Yup, it's a cop," he announced. "Probably smelled your farts, Barger."

"Either that or one of your tampons," I answered. We eased out the fear in dirty jokes that we threw like stones at each other.

"We could really be in for it. What if he just went for backup?" asked Macek, still worried and pale. "He could come back, ya know. Remember the night with the comic books?"

"Cops don't go for help; they use their radios, you wienie."

"Well I'm getting out of here." Macek headed for the back door. I grabbed him at the hallway.

"Easy, Macek. We gotta check it out first, then all slide out fast and quiet."

"Okay, okay!" But he wasn't okay. Neither was I. That big knot was back in my stomach and I wanted to run. Run, run, run. But I laughed. "We'll let the superhero lead us." I gestured toward the swaggering Taylor.

And so we crept out to face the sun and the unknown, Taylor leading followed by Billy then Macek and me. The lot behind the building was empty and we crossed quickly to the brush and dropped down the low hill to Bluff Road. We walked the sidewalk back up the hill and through the neighborhood to our homes.

We wore out the topic of the nosy police car without finding a good reason for him to be there. We finally agreed that it was just coincidence, and in two days we were back on the bandstand where we staged performances to a friendly crowd. We were in the midst of a butchered Gettysburg address by Billy "Abe" Anderson when Taylor got restless. I saw him drift into the shadows then circle back with his hand in his pockets.

"We got to do something."

"Like what, Taylor?" Billy said.

"I don't know. We were going to get some other guys in with us and have some parties and such."

"Who you got in mind?"

"I don't know anybody, you know, really cool."

"How about Macek's sister?" Billy snickered. "I wouldn't mind getting her in the dark."

"My sister? That is sick!" And he flipped the universal bird in Billy's direction.

"Speaking of sisters, Macek, is she the one who taught you to flip the bird?"

"What?" Macek asked, his face confused. He flipped a lame bird at us, his hand wadded into a tight little white-knuckle fist with the thumb folded across it as if holding it together. Protruding from the fist at ninety degrees was a pudgy middle finger.

"You call *that* the bird?" Taylor said with a laugh.

"*This* is the bird," Billy said, standing his middle finger straight up with the other fingers bent at the second joint. The palm of his hand faced him and was flat, the thumb out to the side. It was an icon for all birds I'd seen flipped, a model of perfection.

Macek was unimpressed. "Yeah, so?"

"Show us yours again."

Self-consciously, Macek flipped his lame bird at our collective faces again. And again we laughed shamelessly.

"See what I mean? Compare." Billy flew his magnificent bird once more. It was an eagle soaring above a plucked chicken. We laughed and laughed.

Then I heard it again. Rubber crushing rocks.

"Cops!" I hissed.

This time Billy wasn't cool. It was as if he used up all his bluster and confidence last time. He rushed for the door. I ran to the peephole and saw the blue and white fender pass the side of the building. The cop was driving around back. I ran, hitting the lights I passed. I got to the door at the same time the others did and landed against it with my shoulder. "He's driving around back!"

The tires stopped. The engine stopped. A door opened. I yanked open the closet door to my left, the closet we had used for all our trash. It was about the size of our apartment bathroom and piled deep with cardboard and paper. I pushed the others in, closed the door, and swam for the bottom. The floor was damp and someone kept putting his foot in my face, but I burrowed deeper and pulled musty paper over me.

The cop was thorough. He tested the knob and found the unlocked door. We could hear the shuffle of his shoes as he walked in. He clip-clopped down the hall, his coat brushing the closet door. I mentally followed his footsteps through the whole building.

I also began composing my excuse. If caught I was not going to stand lame-faced and stupid before some cop like I did in the railroad yard. He didn't know anything about us or what we were doing here. The first option, of course, was to tell the truth and bleed all over the floor with explanations of the cleanup work we did and that we didn't break anything, and that we were just having fun.

My experience with grown-ups, however, told me that the playing stupid routine that had worked in the railroad yard was not apt to work again. Then I remembered reading a book about a boy who had chased a lost cat into an abandoned house and discovered a gang of thieves. It had been a silly kid detective story, but the idea was sound. We were just chasing Macek's cat, and it had run into this building. The door was left open, of course. Why were we hiding? We knew this was off-limits, and we didn't know that it was a policeman and we were scared. Sometimes it doesn't pay to act grown up.

The heavy clip-clop of shoes on the tile floor walked back to the closet and paused. An eternity passed. The doorknob rattled and suddenly the door opened. The light of truth and justice seemed to burn away the layers of cardboard and paper. I could feel the cop's stare against my back, and I wondered if the others felt as trapped and naked as I. We lay waiting, fighting the urge to scream, "I surrender!" How were the others so brave, so cool? I couldn't stand it.

Miraculously, the closet door closed. The cop was walking away. Then I heard the door to the outside open and close, then the car door. Gravel met rubber. Freedom. Escape.

My body had been arched in a crescent of fear the whole time, and when I relaxed I found the floor cool and comforting on my cheek. I shivered and trembled like a bird that smacked into a window. I couldn't breath. There wasn't enough air. Perhaps in the whole world there wasn't enough air.

"Let's get the hell outta here!" Macek was on his feet in a cloud of paper and panic. Faint light tumbled into the room so it looked like a gerbil cage.

Taylor stood up and laughed. "Scared ya, huh, Macek?"

Behind Macek, the papers rustled and then erupted. "Yah!!" yelled Billy. Macek dashed into the hall and hit the door with both hands. It didn't budge, even when he turned the knob.

"The door's stuck!" he cried.

"Relax, man. The cop is gone," said Taylor. "What a wienie."

"I told you, the door is stuck." For emphasis Macek put his shoulder against it and bumped it three times.

Billy spilled into the hall all excitement and life. "Shit! That was scary, but kinda cool, huh? That cop was right there two feet from us and couldn't see us." He nearly danced.

"Billy, the door's stuck, you moron!" Macek was still slamming his shoulder against the metal door. I thought he was going to cry.

Taylor pushed him away and tried a few times. The talking stopped and even Billy grew still. Staring like our eyes were magic, we wished silently for the door to swing open to the bright sun and clean air.

"The padlock," I said, flatly.

"What?" Billy asked.

"He padlocked the door."

"No," said Macek. I could hear panic in that one word. He sank to the floor with his back against the sealed gate to freedom. Billy flicked his light on and off. "Might as well have got caught."

"Yeah, we're in jail anyway," said Taylor

"The front door!" Billy yelled. It was a race down the hall with slapping sneakers and bobbing lights. We pushed and rattled the double doors, each taking a turn. Also padlocked.

"My gram's going to wring my neck," said Billy. "My name is mud."

"My dad will use his belt," said Macek.

I could only imagine my mom's anger then terror when I didn't come home on time. She would search alone then call my brother. After that she'd call the police and we would hear the sirens as the manhunt began. All because I had to have this stupid hangout. I was just a dumb kid and I should have left it alone. The fort in the gully would have been fine. Safe and second-rate, but fine.

"Guess we'll have to break a window," offered Taylor.

Three long faces looked at Taylor then followed the beam of his light to a single painted window beside the front door.

"What if someone hears?" asked Macek.

"What if we never get out of here?" Billy seconded.

"You're a bunch of wimps!" Taylor scoffed, then smashed his foot through the glass and punched out the jagged shards around the edges. He climbed up on the sill and kicked again and again at the plywood cover. It bent and cracked then the nails gave way. We were in the bushes behind the club before I breathed again. Taylor had a cut on his ankle and all of us had scrapes from the nails and the ragged plywood. No one complained. We just lay in the weeds and stared at our club that almost turned prison.

I wanted to read their thoughts so I could measure my own. I wanted to say how scary that had been and that I hated the club. I wanted to hear them admit that they too wanted to wet their pants or already had. I wanted to be home in bed reading comics. Suddenly I hated the three friends who lay there silent in the fire-weed waiting to grow up.

"How are we going to get in again?" It was Billy, and I admired and loathed his confidence.

"Are you kidding?" I asked. "It's over. We can't go back in there. Are you crazy?"

"Come on, Sam," Billy begged, "you wanted this. You started this whole thing and it's great. Tell him, Taylor."

"We can't let a little thing like a lock stop us. One crowbar and 'pop' it's gone. No sweat!"

I didn't want this, this positive let's-go-for-it attitude. It was over and I wanted out. Why were they trying to force me into the hole I had dug. "What about the cops?" I asked.

"We'll wait a few days and then we'll come back," I heard Billy say, "with our own padlock."

Just to be safe, we had to avoid the club for a while. For a week it sat dark and abandoned as we ducked at every patrol car or passing MP on his way to the base. We were convinced by the panicky logic of the guilty that our faces were recognizable and a trap had surely been set for us back at the Caribou Club. It would have been easy and safe to move on and forget the club. But this summer wasn't about safe and easy. This was a summer of change and new and different. Mixed in with that was a bit of danger and trespass.

The Caribou Club wouldn't let go of me, and time wore down my fear faster than I would have imagined. Just as I never would have imagined that by the end of that summer the raid on the railroad yard and the stolen comics would seem like small potatoes.

Chapter 12

Billy and I were riding bikes when I realized we had to replace the lock on the Caribou Club. "You know, Billy," I said, cautiously riding one-handed down the middle of an empty street, "I think it's time we took our hangout back from that cop. It's not his any more than it's ours. Let's go to the hardware store."

"Sounds good to me!" he said, and started a U-turn back to the shopping center on Bluff Road just four blocks from the club. I had money from odd jobs and lawn mowing so I bought a solid padlock and hasp. Billy rode home for a hammer and crowbar and some nails.

We cruised the lot on our bikes trying to look like a couple kids just riding around. Then we zipped around the back of the building and dropped our bikes in the grass. The crowbar took the lock right off the door, but the staple came with it. "Crap," whispered Billy, "what now?"

"Don't sweat the small stuff," I bragged. Taking one of the biggest nails from Billy's bag, I drove it into one of the screw holes, then bent it over. Twice we stopped our work and hid because we thought we heard someone coming, but we were alone.

"I hope this works," I muttered.

In less time than it took to get the lock off, I had our new one on. The Caribou Club was ours. We only had time for a quick inspection before Billy had to check in at home, but we were feeling pretty good about things when we left.

On the way home I was feeling cocky and tried to jump the curb from the street onto the sidewalk by running straight at it on the bike and lifting the handlebars at the last instant. My timing was off or I didn't lift enough because my wheel hit the curb straight on and I hit my hands and head straight on the concrete. My left cheek bumped the rough curb and I could hardly see through the blur of pain.

I wanted to cry, and I would have, but a car full of high school boys passed and hooted, "OOHH NOO!!" I ignored them as they rattled past.

They deserved nothing from me, especially not my tears. So I choked on them even though my cheek was swelling and blood ran from both hands and a knee. The front fork with the wheel still attached was bent at a ninety-degree angle to the rest of the bike.

"Are you okay?" asked a voice that I knew too well, a voice I didn't want to hear at all, not now, not any day I could think of. Mr. Perfect. Allen. His hand touched my arm and my shame should have burned his fingers. I had no honor or armor to face him with. I turned my head and rubbed my tears with blood from my hand and the two salty liquids mixed and stung my eyes like vinegar.

I knew he could see that I was crying, that I was hurt and ashamed. But his voice was kind. "Man, I didn't think you'd get up from that one. You are one tough rider, Sam."

"I . . . I fall a lot." I wished I had a long sleeve to wipe my nose on but I didn't, so I wiped it on my bare arm.

My bike lay across the curb and with the front fork bent so it pointed to the sky with the front wheel spinning slowly and squeaking. Allen leaned past me and lifted my bike with one hand and studied the damage.

He whistled. "Here's your problem, metal fatigue. See where the fork's bent over?"

"What's metal fatigue?" Why did this guy have to be so nice? He was supposed to be the Evil One that had captured my true love. The kind of guy who would run me over, not pick me up and tell me my bike had metal fatigue.

"It just means the metal is old and tired, not as strong as it used to be, like a rotten chunk of wood. It couldn't take the stress of hitting that curb. It happened to the leaf spring in my car, and it just broke one day. Scared me to death."

"Really?" I said, but I meant, "*You* were scared? You, Mr. Perfect?"

He brushed off my back without answering and then scooped up the bike. A left hand reached without effort into the car and snagged the keys, popped the trunk, and loaded my bent bicycle.

"Hop in, I'll give you a lift." I stumbled helplessly into the car. I wasn't weak from the fall, just unable to resist the warm kindness that he presented like a gift that only he could give. I sat once more in the shiny '56 Chevy, trying to sit so that I didn't bleed on anything and spoil the perfection.

"Why don't you let me borrow that bike and stick another fork on it for you."

"I can't afford a new fork."

"Who can? I've got a couple old bikes at home. I bet one of those will fit. It wasn't that long ago that I was riding a bike to get around just like you." He seemed determined to make me feel small and useless by doing for me all those things I could not do myself. I wanted to strongly and forcefully say no, that I could fix it myself, but I couldn't actually fix it myself. I knew that, he knew that. But I let my pride speak anyway. "I can fix it myself."

"Oh, I figure with you not having a dad and all, you wouldn't have the tools." He watched the street and the people slowing down to admire his car. He was careful not to look at me while I thought it over like he knew that I would find it too easy to say yes to him.

"Yeah, I guess I don't really."

"Great! What's your apartment number? I'll drop her by when she's rolling again." He called the bike "her," and I knew he treated things that way, trusting that if he were nice to them and gentle that he could fix anything he touched. I knew it would be several days before the bike came home, and I even imagined, when well away from his charm and charisma, that I might never see my bike again. Sure, it was only secondhand, but it was all I had.

The next morning it didn't matter because, not only was I bruised and sore, but I was also vomiting up everything I ate and drank and ached with a torturous fever. Summer flu landed with both feet on my stomach.

It was in this crumpled state that I met Janice, one of my sister's friends. She was loud, small with impish curly hair and a giggly voice that sounded like she was talking and trying to keep from laughing at the same time. She was older than me but looked and acted young, so I guess I felt confident around her. She was hanging around the apartment that week and was the one that would bring me tissues and cool washrags. On the third day, she sat on my bed and touched my black and blue cheek as she pressed damp washrags against my head so that cold water ran down my neck and chilled me beneath my fever.

"I'm studying to be a nurse," she said.

"Really?"

"Yeah and you're my first patient. I think it's good to practice. I mean . . . I want to be ready."

"Can I have some water?" She brought the water and looked down at me as I drank. It was hard to drink lying down and the water spilled down my shirt.

"You've just got to have a straw." And away she went to the kitchen and returned with a drinking straw. "Don't you think it would be great working in a big hospital, taking care of people? Really doing something good, you know. It's going to be so groovy."

Janice was still talking when I dozed off, and when I woke from my nap she had fallen asleep beside me. My fever had broken, and I lay stinking and clammy in my sickbed. I managed to open a comic and read without waking her. I had never been this close to a sleeping girl (other than my sister) and it was exciting and scary, like when I snared my first rabbit.

When she awoke a few minutes later she tried to act like she wasn't embarrassed.

"What ya doin'?" she asked.

"Comics . . . readin' comics."

She grabbed a *Richie Rich*. "This is my favorite." And she lay on the corner of my pillow and read comics with me until somehow our hands were crushed together on the edge of a *Captain America* that I was just starting, and she was reading over my arm.

"We're holding hands, you know," she said after the third page.

"Uh-uh."

"Do you like that?"

"Uh, sure," I choked out. I got through two pages without reading a word. A new fever had struck me. She leaned close, and she smelled like soap, not clean, just like soap. I thought of how gross my breath must smell after twelve hours of vomiting. Then my lips were on her cheek. They seemed to paralyze her entire body until I wondered, Did that cheek have no feeling? If she slapped me I might wet myself or vomit, but she didn't, then I turned and kissed her on the lips.

We stayed there frozen for a while. I still gripped the *Captain America* comic as if I were reading it, my sweaty hands seeping through the pages. My limbs did not move, but my heart revved like I was halfway through the hundred-yard dash, and each of my bones had become a great rod of fire seething like magma beneath my fragile crust.

Here was passion, hampered only by the crick in my neck and a total lack of direction. What was I supposed to do besides kiss her?

"What are you two doing in there? You making out with my little brother?" Mary's voice crashed through my door like the bolts from a witch's wand, and the spell was broken. My magma cooled, and Janice left giggling. I lay, still without moving, and imagined the right words and motions to carry this princess into a kingdom where I was the king and knew how to kiss.

Then, without warning, a great spasm shook me and I vomited into the trashcan beside my bed. I felt much better after that, and slept until well past dinner.

I didn't see Janice again that summer, though I thought of her often, and sometimes in a restroom or a store or maybe standing in line at the movie, I would smell her soap smell and it would awaken an appetite in me that I could not understand.

With my flu gone and inspired by my bedroom encounter with Janice, I went in search of similar excitement: excitement in some ways dangerous. Girls. Shirley and Janice had awakened me to the knowledge that there was magic beneath those jeans and T-shirts. Images of girls came to me often now, and my vivid imagination outlined their limbs and the shape of their lips until I thought I would go insane.

On the first hot day of July, Taylor and I were reading comics in Macek's bedroom while he finished his chores. The comics were forgotten when we spotted Macek's fifteen-year-old sister, Kathy, lying out on a blanket in their backyard.

"Gosh, would you look at that?" asked Taylor. "WOW!"

"Oh yeah! I'd give a hundred bucks to just be the blanket," I panted, not turning my eyes from her chest, rising and falling with a beguiling rhythm.

Kathy was curvy and blond and she lay that day on a blue cotton blanket centered in the blotchy green lawn. Cutoff jeans hugged the roundness of her rump, teasing us with the white trim of her panties when she lay on her stomach. Luckily, she lacked the patience for extended sunbathing and rolled often to her back, her breasts forming tempting mounds beneath her tank top.

Macek roamed in from finishing his chores. "Hey, guys, what's doin'?" he asked.

"Checking out your sister," Taylor bragged.

"Oh no, is she out sunbathing?" Then he jerked open the window and yelled, "Gross! Put some clothes on!"

Kathy rolled to her stomach and flipped the bird in our direction. I saw a flash of white panty as she settled her hips into the blanket, a gift to a silent admirer. The finger was just for Macek.

"You guys are sick," Macek chided. "I can't believe you're spying on my sister."

"Looks pretty good to me. Heh, heh, heh!" Taylor taunted. "Where's Carol?"

"She's comin' over, you'll see. And . . ." he grinned, "I heard Kathy tell her to bring her bikini."

I couldn't help but ask, "Who's Carol?"

Taylor laughed. "Why, that's Macek's dream girl. Did I mention she doesn't know he exists?"

"We are talking one crazy skin flick right here in my backyard," said Macek.

"I've got a plan," said Taylor, not taking his eyes off of Macek's sister.

"I'll bet."

"No, really, listen. We can get a look at more than just the bikinis."

I caught his thinking. "You mean while they're changing."

"Yeah, while they're changing! Come on!" Once more Taylor would lead us into the dangerous off-limits zone of life. "Keep watch," he ordered, and I waited in the hall as he entered Kathy's bedroom and raised the blinds about three inches, creating a gap through which we could peak. Safely outside, we found a spot behind the fuel tank and by standing on tiptoe we could look through the window and into a large mirror above the dresser. Perfect view.

Macek muttered his disgust that we were so interested in his sister.

We were waiting on the front steps when Carol appeared. She swayed her hips as she walked toward us. Macek grew silent in awe. Then she passed us, and ran giggling into the house with Kathy. Taylor and I jumped up and ran around the corner of the house, leaping geraniums and trampling pansies as we raced to be first to pick balcony seats. Macek stayed on the porch alone.

With one foot on the crossbar of the fuel tank platform and a white-knuckled hand on the vent pipe, I had a precarious but unobstructed view of heaven. I noticed someone had opened the window, so I held my breath. Just then Kathy stepped in front of the mirror right on cue, as if she had attended rehearsals I'd held in my mind for the last ten minutes. Brushing back her hair, she crossed her arms, grasped the hem of her tank top, and pulled it up past her bra and away from her body with a flip of her head. I was embarrassed being there spying on her, but at the same time, I couldn't resist. The bra, I thought desperately. Now the bra!

Kathy reached both hands back to the clasp at the center of her back, making chicken wings of her shoulders. As her fingers grasped the clasp, a wind roared in my ears . . .

. . . and a water balloon came crashing through my fantasy. The tumbling yellow ball arced across my view into the window, hit the edge of the frame, and exploded, spraying water into the bedroom. I was left with a cruel image of Kathy, arms across her chest, face filled with horror.

I would never forget that face, no matter how many months passed, and when I saw it I was ashamed. Macek tried to make up to Taylor and me by buying us pop with his paper route money, but we couldn't tell him where it hurt, and he couldn't get over that delicious joy of his prank.

When I slunk back home that day, I saw Melissa sitting on

the down end of a teeter-totter with her feet in a puddle, trying to make her tiny body weightless enough to bounce up and down. But the teeter-totter would not lift even her without help.

"Hi, Sam," she said, "your sister is babysitting me."

It was late so I asked, "Where is she?" Some babysitter. I recognized the yellow Plymouth that her current boyfriend drove.

"Inthide. She washed my hair."

"I see that and she gave you braids. Those are nice."

"I'm seesawing?"

"You need two people to seesaw."

"You could help me."

"I've got to go home."

She was irresistible without knowing it, with her hair clean and a face free of playground dirt, she didn't need to plead. I was learning to look past the distracting growth above her eyes.

"Okay." I pushed down on the seesaw and sent her toward the sky where she fearlessly reached up with both hands toward heaven. Up and down she went, rising and falling to the rusty tune of the grinding metal mechanism.

"Teeter-totter, bread and water, wash your face in dirty water," I sang unconsciously.

"That's a silly song."

I chuckled. "No, it's magic and you must sing it when you ride the seesaw," I said, feeling suddenly wise and strong. I kept pumping the seesaw until she knew the rhyme, and I left her singing a song meant for two.

I went to bed with jumbled emotions. I was thinking of girls with bare backs and a tumbling yellow balloon. But then I was thinking about little Melissa sitting on the teeter-totter. Someday would she have boys sneaking around to see her in a bikini? I was finding girls to be more fascinating than ever and at the same time more confusing. I was also feeing guilty about the times I made fun of Melissa and feeling sorry that she might someday grow up and think she was ugly.

But for now she was happy sitting there singing, "Teeter-totter, bread and water, wash your face in dirty water." And I was happy too.

Chapter 13

Iwasn't home when Allen brought back my bike and told my mother the story I had kept from her. I kept most things from her then. Not out of sneakiness, but because it seemed that such knowing was the only ownership that I could claim. The shame of the broken bike was mine as much as the first kiss from an older girl was. Shared, they were no longer precious.

"So, young man," she asked that night at dinner, "who is this Allen character that fixed your bike?"

"Just a guy who helped me out."

"Where did you meet him? Isn't he kinda old for you to be friends with?"

"He's a senior," declared Mary, "and so cute."

I shook my head. "He's not my friend, and he has a girlfriend, Mary."

"Sam, you need to hang out with kids your own age and don't take any more rides with people I don't know." She seemed worried, so I vowed to make sure she learned less about my friends and me.

When Macek and Taylor showed up after dinner, they were all whispers and nods.

"Hey, guys, what's up?" I asked.

"Come on," ordered Taylor, nodding his head away from the apartment and out toward the world.

"Give me five minutes. I'll meet you downstairs."

The guys split, clomping down the stairs to the sunlight. Taylor turned at the bottom. "Hurry up, Barger!" he shouted.

I dashed to my room and did the stuff-and-shuffle so it looked like I cleaned it, then I raced back to the kitchen and ran hot water over the dinner dishes, and wiped the table with a cold dishrag.

"Mom, I'm going out for a while," I called down the hall. "I got my chores done." Without waiting for a reply, I was gone into the summer evening.

Macek and Taylor were talking about water ballooning cars again. In their eyes it was the height of the summer. I got the knot in my gut again and was glad when Billy rode up on his bike with excitement all over his face and changed the subject.

"I've got an idea," he said in a voice that made us all listen. Standing like he was giving a prepared speech in class, Billy looked at each of us and said the magic words, "Do you want to ride in a brand-new, supercharged, burgundy Corvette Stingray fastback?"

"What's burgundy?" asked Taylor.

"Purple, stupid," I said. "Who's going to give us a ride?"

"My neighbor." Billy spoke with such uncommon confidence that skepticism lost out to anticipation and we rushed on, pumping Billy for details as we went.

Billy led us to a house in his neighborhood where, true to his word, a burgundy Corvette glistened in the driveway. It hovered above the oil-stained pavement like a spaceship, all chrome and power. The car seemed to glow with extraterrestrial energy that could transport its passengers into another atmosphere and bring them back bigger and wiser. Manlike.

For the first time in a week, I wasn't thinking about a white Chrysler and a water balloon or the sound of the cop walking through the Caribou Club.

"Wow!" Macek gasped. "Can you believe it? Look at the paint. It looks wet, like you could reach your hand right into it."

"Someday," Taylor bragged, "when I get my license I'm going to get a red one."

"Yeah, right! You couldn't buy the gas for this," I said, squatting down to peer at the chrome exhaust. No one touched the car. It was as if a force field surrounded it.

"You know the guy who owns this?" Taylor asked.

Billy nodded.

"Nice looking ride, isn't it boys." A man appeared from the side of the house surprising us. "I bet you'd like a ride in her, wouldn't you?"

We jumped back nodding and grinning. "Hey, Mr. Martin," Billy said, "I brought my buddies over to look at your car."

"Oh, I thought maybe someone was trying to steal it," he said with a laugh. He was tall and lean, with oiled-back hair, and smelled strongly of cologne. The kind of guy my dad would have called "slick."

"Could we?" I asked.

"If you're friends of Billy, it's okay by me." Mom's voice popped unwanted into my head, "Don't take rides with people I don't know." Obviously, this didn't count. This was Billy's neighbor. Plus, I *had* to ride in that car. Fear of the unknown was becoming more of a spice than a poison these days. I had become the car crasher, magazine stealer, kisser of older girls.

Mr. Martin grinned at our eagerness, as if he knew his beautiful car was filling our afternoon to the brim with happiness. "So you boys going to wash my car for me in trade for a ride?"

"Looks pretty clean to me," volunteered Macek.

"Oh, not this baby. I'm the only one who cleans the 'Vette," he said, laughing again. "That one!" He pointed to an old station wagon coated in dust and mud. "Took that one fishing down on the Kenai last weekend; she needs a bath."

"Let's get to it, boys!" Billy said, jumping to the task. Soon we had buckets and suds and rags, all of us eager to get that car clean. It was the fastest chore completed in my life.

Once finished, we dried off and lined up for the ride. "One at a time!" Mr. Martin said. "It's a two-seater."

Taylor grabbed a door handle and jumped in first.

The driver smiled at him and slid silently behind the wheel, and with no blast of noise or belch of smoke when the engine came to life, the Corvette hummed and floated out of the driveway. The car hesitated a second, then launched with a wisp of exhaust and a throaty rumble that carried it beyond our view around a distant corner. Five minutes later they were back: the grinning driver and a goggle-eyed kid riding in a spaceship on wheels.

"Don't say a word!" I instructed Taylor as he climbed out of the cockpit, as if his words alone could soil the perfection of sunlight on chrome and paint. "Don't ruin it for the rest of us."

"Nuts. But it was so—"

"Shut up!" I insisted.

Macek was about to wet his pants with excitement, so I let him go next. I didn't even look inside when the door opened. I wanted no preview of my ride. I wanted the whole experience to be a unique and pure peek into the future.

When Macek returned, Billy and I stood with our hands in the pockets of our jeans. We looked at each other grinning, then, "Go ahead," he offered. I jumped in, as if at any moment my mother or a cop would swoop in and ruin this best of moments.

"Nice to meet you," Mr. Martin said, extending his hand. I took it in a firm handshake.

"Sam Barger," I answered, as I settled myself into the passenger seat.

As Mr. Martin grabbed the shifter and pumped the gas, I turned my attention to the cockpit. I couldn't believe it. I'd seen pictures of the tight cockpit of a racing car, and I felt like that's where I was. The leather bucket seat wrapped around me, and the dash was bright with chrome and gauges. I sucked in a delicious noseful of new car smell.

I tried to picture myself as I was at that instant, sitting inside that beautiful car. But it made me feel grimy and poorly dressed, so instead I made a face at the trio outside the window.

The engine roared, quieter inside than outside the car. A giant hand seemed to slap me on the chest as the car sank slightly, then surged through the flat dimensions of cars and houses painted on flat canvas along our path. The speedometer hit ninety before Mr. Martin finally let off the gas and punched my knee lightly. "You ever feel such power? Pretty sweet isn't it?"

"Nice car," I managed to squeak out as we drifted around the corner and glided onto Hollywood Drive. When we catapulted past the Big G Drive-In and on past the Caribou Club, I gasped like the air was gone from the car. In the other cars on the street, crude and clumsy next to us, drivers turned their heads to gawk. I simmered in a sauce of feelings; I wanted to wave like a parade grand marshal, but I was still trying to catch my breath and was feeling glad none of the faces were familiar.

In a breath, if I took one, the ride was over, and I had to open the door, breaking the seal on my time machine. I had traveled into the future and now was returned to my life as a kid. I was still just a boy in jeans and a T-shirt standing in front of Mr. Martin's house.

"Sure beats walking, doesn't it," Taylor said, an injection of reality.

"I hope they make it illegal for you to ever own a car like this," I said, surprised at the mean tone of my voice.

The roar of the Corvette ended our duel, and I tried to laugh as we watched Billy disappear in the glare of sunlight off the rear window of his dream car. I wanted to see his face but had to settle for imagining him sinking back in the seat, swallowed by the ecstasy.

It would have been perfect for me and Billy to walk home together, reliving those precious minutes we each spent in the stratosphere, but I couldn't risk getting home late. One of the gauges in the Corvette was a clock, and it was pushing up on Mom's precise 9:00 PM curfew when we pulled into Mr. Martin's driveway. I couldn't stand being grounded this week, so I left Billy to savor his ride alone. Tomorrow would come soon enough.

That night, I couldn't bury the image of that car ride, the smells, the sounds, the feeling of being pressed back into the seat as we accelerated. Over and over, I pictured Billy and me riding away in a space car that lifted off the street and disappeared into the darkness.

"Sam! Wake up!"

My eyes snapped open and my mother's worried face filled my vision. "Sam, wake up. Something terrible has happened."

Chapter 14

Alarms went off in my brain, and I automatically started searching for lies. I immediately went back to the day Dad had his first attack, but he was already dead. He couldn't die twice. So this had to be about me.

"What's the matter?" I mumbled, trying to think straight.

Mom sat on the edge of the bed. "It's about your friend, Billy."

The alarms went off again. Billy! He's dead. Dying, dead, died.

"His grandmother just called," she continued. "He didn't come home tonight and she's worried sick. She called all the Bargers on Government Hill looking for you. Do you know where he is?"

"What? Uh, no." Was there a lie needed here? "What time is it?"

"Three in the morning."

Mom must be worried big-time to wake me up in the middle of the night. I had learned that much in my short life. Every mom thinks every kid is her kid. What happens to one kid happens to all of us, even if that kid is a total stranger. I wasn't the one missing, but it didn't make any difference to her.

For once, I told her most everything. I told about riding in Mr. Martin's Corvette without her permission. I told her about places Billy and I usually rode our bikes. I told her about the gully where we'd built our lean-to, and about sneaking into the rail yard. I told her a lot, but I didn't tell her everything. She didn't need to know about the Caribou Club. Not yet.

After I cleared my conscience, she left and I tried to go back to sleep. But it was impossible. My brain imagining what might have happened to Billy.

The next day there were police to talk to. Instead of talking at home, they took me to the police station downtown. At first it was cool riding in a police car, but then I started to worry about all the laws I had probably broken this summer. Did they know somehow? I was glad when Joe drove across town to check on me and be at my side during the interview. He even gave me a hug.

A serious and nervous young cop about Joe's age took me into an office and gave me a Coke. He asked my full name and age then looked at the tabletop and asked, "What about this Mr. Martin? Did he touch you? Did he give you presents?"

"What?"

"I'm sorry, kid. I understand that you boys were at the home of Billy's neighbor, Mr. Martin, and that he gave you all rides in his car."

"Yeah, he did. So?"

"And these car rides. You were alone with him, one at a time? Is that right?"

"Well, a Corvette Stingray is a two-seater, sir. So what?"

"So, did Mr. Martin touch you or say anything he shouldn't

have? You know." The cop looked helplessly at Joe, as if he could explain it to me, this thing he was hinting at. But I understood.

I shook my head. "It wasn't like that. Mr. Martin was just a friendly guy with a cool car. It was nice of him to give us rides. That's all I know." That's all I wanted to know.

"Why are you asking about Mr. Martin?" I asked. "He's a friend of Billy's; he's a neighbor. You should be looking for Billy. Something must have happened to him." Something had happened all right; I just couldn't figure what.

I had to tell my story over and over again, until the emotion of my missing friend was worn away in the telling, like a bad joke that isn't funny the second time around. In the end I was left with just my confusion and Taylor and Macek as my only friends.

On the way home from the police station, I tried to imagine where Billy could be, but it was beyond me. I replayed the events of the evening, looking for the answers to everybody's questions. The cops seemed to think Mr. Martin was the answer to their question, and I had to admit, "Slick" was sort of weird. What kind of guy would give rides to neighbor kids instead of cruising for beautiful women in that rolling chick magnet of a Corvette? Maybe I had it all wrong. And worse, maybe Billy was gone for good. Maybe.

A Corvette pulled beside us at a stoplight, and I felt my stomach coil into a tight twist. I couldn't look at the driver and I hated that car that Billy would have loved. As the car moved away from us down a side street, I remembered Billy rising from the ground with his arms outstretched that time we saw the 'Vette go by.

For the second night in a row I hardly slept. Why didn't we go to the movie that day, instead of to Mr. Martin's? If only.

The next morning I called Macek. "You talk to the cops?"

"Yeah. Me and Taylor both."

"Did you tell them about the Caribou Club?"

"No way. I'm no fink!"

I didn't trust him anymore. "What *did* you tell them then? They asked me a ton of questions. Come on, man!"

"Nothin'. Really nothin'. Just a bunch of made-up stuff."

"You didn't tell them about the fort or the water balloons? You didn't tell them about riding in Mr. Martin's 'Vette?"

"Well, I had to tell 'em about that. That guy was a weirdo. My dad says he's got a record and everything. We told the cops how Billy was hanging around his place last time we saw him."

"Whose place?"

"Martin's place. I'm sure he's got Billy. My dad says anybody that's nice to kids like us is probably a pervert."

I couldn't believe my ears so I just hung up the phone and stared at the wall. With Macek telling the cops things like that, no wonder the cops were all over Mr. Martin. No wonder they thought the worst.

Once again I was doubting myself. Was it possible? Could Mr. Martin have kidnapped Billy? He seemed like a nice guy, but then people always said stuff like that about psychos, didn't they? And if it wasn't Mr. Martin, then where was Billy? The wheels in my brain started turning again, once I quit doubting myself. I was pretty sure something made Billy run away from home. And that meant one thing: I knew where he was.

I was supposed to stay home where Mary could keep an eye on me. Since Billy went missing, my mom didn't want me out of sight. But I had to get out of there. Had to take some action. And I figured I had enough dope on Mary to make her cover for me. I was halfway down the front stairs when she saw me leaving.

"You little sneak! Get back up here. If you so much as look out that front door, Mom will have us both sent to the salt mines." Mary was at her tough, motherly best. "I'm not getting grounded just because you and your stupid friends can't stay out of trouble."

Ignoring her, I jumped on my bike and rode standing up most of the way to the Caribou Club. We never approached the club directly and always left the brush along the street undisturbed, but this time I crashed on through and entered from the street side of the club, not caring that someone might see me.

With all the police interrogations and worried parents, I hadn't spoken one word about the club. It wasn't on purpose, at least on my part; just no one had thought of it. Maybe hiding and lying were becoming second nature. Billy could be there. I couldn't figure out why or what might have happened to him, but that was where he would be if he ran off. I knew it. I was so sure that I stopped and bought him an Almond Joy on my way.

When I got to the club the padlock was still in place and locked. That wasn't good. I had given Billy a key, but he wouldn't have been able to lock it again from the inside. Then I remembered the broken window we escaped through when the cop locked the door on us. I ran around the building, but the broken window was covered from the outside with a scrap like we had left. I walked fearfully around the building and peeked in all the dirty windows. No sign of Billy, so I gave up and walked home.

"Wait up, Barger!" Taylor and Macek were trudging up the road from the other direction. They broke into a run when they saw me.

"Wait up, Barger!" Taylor called again. "What happened to you?"

I stopped and tried to look casual, but I had a sour taste in my mouth. "What do you want?"

"Whoa, man," said Macek. "What's your problem? After you asked if we'd talked to the cops about the club, it hit me."

"Yeah," added Taylor, "we split as soon as I could get away. Maybe Billy went there to hide out from something."

"Forget it. I was just there. Billy's not at the Caribou Club. Now just leave me alone." I started walking home again.

"Wait up," Macek said. "You went to the club alone?"

"Yeah, what of it?" I kept walking, talking over my shoulder. "And besides, I thought you said Mr. Martin had done Billy in."

"We just said that stuff about Martin to keep the cops off our backs," Taylor answered.

"That's just great," I sneered. "Look, I don't know what happened, but you shouldn't have lied about Mr. Martin. He was nice to us."

A flicker of something passed over their faces. Guilt? Doubt? Then Macek said, "Man, Taylor, you shouldn't have lied!"

"Oh yeah, Macek, I'm the one who lied," Taylor countered. "And you were Mr. Honesty!"

As I walked away Macek called to me, "Hey, Sam, wait a minute! You wanna go spy on the cops searching the gully?"

Taylor pleaded, "Hey, Sam, I'm sorry, man."

"Yeah, double for me," Macek added.

I was lonely, missing Billy, and another time I might have been tempted to join them just for the company, like I had two months ago. Instead I kept my mouth shut and kept walking.

Chapter 15

The next day there was still no news of Billy. The cops had called his grandma and she had called Mom to keep her in the know. The search had started in Billy's backyard and spread through the alleys to the abandoned Quonset hut and then on to the gully. All our neighborhood haunts. Apparently, there were some questions about a camp they found there, and after I told Mom it was ours she wanted to keep me close in case the police had questions. She made a deal with me to clean and repair the storage units in the basement so I could make money for school clothes. Her orders were clear: stay close to home and don't leave without permission.

I spent the whole morning tacking up chicken wire on the beat-up storage compartments that lined up like prison cells along one wall of the basement. They were all framed in wood and covered with chicken wire. Some were without doors and others had part of the chicken wire pulled away. My job was to fix the wire and screw the doors back on. Then I had to sweep and haul out any trash.

In the quiet of the musty basement, I sat among the boxes of old canning jars and daydreamed of being somewhere else. My mind wandered back to Billy. Billy in the spotlight singing "I Want to Hold Your Hand." Billy leaping bumps on his bike along the bluff, his straight black hair bouncing. Billy who didn't know how to whistle.

I tried to push out everything that wasn't pretend because I didn't want the real world in my head right then. But the real wouldn't stay out and soon I was stewing on Billy again. I missed him, and rather than bringing me closer to Taylor and Macek, it made me see their shortcomings even more clearly. Macek and Taylor had fear on their minds; fear that it could have been one of them gone missing. It could have been one of them that people would forget even before they knew of them. I had enough fear; I didn't need theirs.

When I was replacing the lightbulb in our storage unit, I suddenly felt like turning loose all my anger and hurt. I was standing on a chair and dropped the bulb. It exploded with a loud pop, and I remembered how Taylor had thrown them in the club. Something snapped and I went out in the hallway and unscrewed two more lightbulbs and stood in the near darkness with them still hot against my hands. I ran the length of the hall, throwing the bulbs over my shoulder one at a time. They exploded like grenades, and I wanted to do more, but I stopped and stared at the shattered glass.

This wasn't me. I didn't want to be like Macek and Taylor. I swept up the mess.

Even that distraction didn't last long and my mind went back to Billy. I remembered the first time I'd seen him riding his banana seat bike. Then I remembered something else. I had ridden past his house the day before and his bike wasn't in the carport. He always parked there, not in the backyard, not on the front lawn, always in the carport. Yet it wasn't there. If it wasn't there, he must have ridden it somewhere. And he hadn't been on his bike when we went to Mr. Martin's house. He had parked it in the carport and walked over. And I had seen fresh bike tracks in the mud behind the Caribou Club!

Billy had been there. I had to go back. I charged up the stairs to the apartment, grabbed some money and the padlock key, and headed for the door. My hand was on the doorknob when Mom came barreling in.

"You're home early!" I nearly shouted.

Mom reached out and took a hold of me like it might be the last time we got to hug.

"Sam, sweetie," she said, and I could tell she was about to cry. "I had to come home and tell you in person. I couldn't do it over the phone. Billy's grandma finally told me the whole story. Billy's dad was killed in Vietnam last week. He was a soldier, you know. Billy had been carrying that around inside him for days before he disappeared. And now he's gone too. Oh, that poor dear lady."

I felt like I was falling back in time. I could taste the sea air and smell the salmon from my last day on the bluff. I could see the cloud of dust hiding the car as it tore out of the yard with the last of my dad in it.

"You might be right about that boy, Sam. Maybe he did run away. Billy might just be out there somewhere lost and hiding and you may be the best bet of finding him." I was halfway out the door when she stopped me long enough to stuff some cookies in a paper sack and press it into my hand.

A half an hour later, I stood alone inside the club and no ambush of cops awaited me. Just quiet darkness. Our kingdom was intact. And even with the door padlocked I was positive that Billy had found a way to get in. I could just feel it. He wasn't dead and he wasn't kidnapped. He was right here in our hangout somewhere.

I turned on what lights I could and called softly, "Billy. Hey, man, you here?"

I roamed through the building and saw and heard nothing, no sign that anyone had been there. Maybe my gut was wrong. I called again as I walked toward the back door. There I paused.

A sound, a tiny rattle, almost not a sound at all, came from over my left shoulder. I froze. Then I heard it again from inside the closet where we hid from the cops. I jerked open the door and jammed my flashlight into the darkness. In the center of the mound of paper and cardboard was a shoe, a single sneaker sticking out of the trash.

"Billy? Is that you?" My voice was soft but still echoed out in the hallway.

The shoe moved. And then another emerged and then jeans and arms. And then Billy Anderson, my best friend, rolled out of the pile of old paper. He shrunk back from me with his arms up as if I might hit him.

"Billy!" My yell echoed through the empty building.

"Sam," was all he said. Then he came to me and we hugged shamelessly.

He began to cry.

"I knew it!" I lied. "I knew you'd be here."

"Where have you been?" he asked. "What took you so long?"

"What do you mean? Why didn't you holler? Didn't you hear me calling you."

"I must have been asleep. But why didn't you come sooner is what I mean. I've been waiting."

This time I cried a little and smiled at my friend, the friend I'd given up on, the friend I'd let the rest of the world take away from me. "I thought . . . they said Mr. Martin did something bad to you."

"What?" He was confused and shaken. "What do you mean, Sam? Who thought what?"

So we sat down and I told him the whole story. How the police and everybody were thinking he'd been kidnapped or something. I told how Mr. Martin was a suspect. I told how I'd already come here once before.

Then he stopped me. "You came here looking for me already?"

"Yeah, yesterday. I came and looked all around the outside, but the lock was still on the door and everything looked tight as we left it. I didn't think you were here."

"I didn't want to be found, not at first," he explained. "And I thought you'd look here right away. So I got in and hid the bike inside, then pried open a window and went back out to lock the lock. I got back in through the window a couple times."

"You been coming and going?"

"Yeah. Yesterday when you were here I was probably down at the railroad yard. Remember that day when we were there? You and that railroad cop." He started laughing.

I had to laugh, too, but I also wanted to scream or something. "What were you doing there? In the railroad yard."

"I was going to jump a train and get out of town. But there were no trains, and I couldn't find a way to do it, so I just came back and waited for you. I knew you'd come."

"Good thing for Mr. Martin you didn't get on that train. They'd arrest him for sure."

"That doesn't make any sense, the cops arresting Mr. Martin. He didn't do anything. He's just a goofy old guy with greasy hair. A nice, goofy old guy with greasy hair. What a bummer."

He shook his head, then changed the subject. "You got any food? I've been eating nothing but candy bars out of the machine at the gas station for days now."

Oh gosh, food. I took out the cookies and I offered them. "So why did you run away? What's the matter?"

Billy was quiet, wolfing down a cookie. The shadows of the Caribou Club surrounded us and I felt chilly. I wanted sunlight. Billy stood and walked out into the ballroom, so I got up and followed him, flipping on the stage lights to make things brighter. He turned and looked at me, right into my eyes. "My dad, he's dead now, like yours."

"But how?" I let him tell it like I didn't know. For some reason, I wanted him to feel like it was fresh to me.

Billy walked to the bandstand and boosted himself up. He seemed unsteady and weak like he might fall any minute. I waited for more. I knew it was his to say.

"I lost my dad."

"He was in the army, right?"

"That's right. And . . . and he was in Vietnam and they killed him."

"Oh, Billy." The heat rose in me like I hadn't heard the news before. Him saying it made it real. "Goddammit!" I yelled. And we sat there staring into the shadows around the stage.

"Sam, it's already like he never was at all."

"Don't say that, Billy. You just gotta hold on to the things you remember. I like to remember this one night I spent with my dad at the beach. He was blowing smoke rings for me. He let me drink some of his coffee—it was sweet and creamy—and he blew a smoke ring that rose past me. It spread wide getting bigger and bigger, then it bent until the ring was broken and there was only a wisp."

I stopped talking and just sat there, remembering. "Smoke rings are like our lives," I continued. "They start out tight and perfect, then they roll and grow and you can't stop them. Can't control them. Sometimes they get thin and twisted until they aren't rings anymore . . . and then they're gone."

It was awhile before Billy said anything. "It seems like everything is so dark now."

I shook my head, trying to shake off the dark mood. "And it stinks, Billy, it does. But it gets better. Slowly. Your smoke ring ain't broken yet."

It was quiet again for a time as I waited for him to say what was in his head.

"I gotta go live with my mom. She's all messed up. That's why I ran away."

"You didn't have to run. You could have told me. I could've helped. But it doesn't matter. You're alive, man. That's good enough for me." Alive, living, lived! I could feel warmth coming into me.

"They want to send me to Oregon. To my mom. But I don't want to live with somebody who hated my dad. I want to stay here."

"I know it feels right, but running away won't work," I heard myself say, like I was some grown-up or something. "You're still a kid. You're stuck."

"I know," he said. "What's it like for you, being without a dad?"

"I don't know. Kinda weird, I guess. It messes things up. You know, like he's just not there, and you feel like he's lookin' over your shoulder. It changes everything. When I was little one time, I couldn't sleep. Lots of times I can't sleep so I make up stories. You know, I pretend I'm someone else, living a different life.

"And one time, I don't know why, I imaged both my parents died and left me an orphan. It was so real it made me cry." I was actually choking up pretty good just telling the story. "Then when my dad actually died and I really was an orphan, I didn't cry at all."

Billy chuckled. "Yeah, I was mad because my mom *didn't* want me to live with her, so I had to come live with Gramma. And now Mom *wants* me to come live with her, but I don't want to. It was like all of it was too much. I had to get the hell out of there."

"And you've just been hanging out here? All this time?"

"Where else could I go? This morning in the railroad yard when I was planning to jump a train, I thought to myself, Then what, Billy Anderson? Where you gonna go? Fairbanks? What are you gonna do in Fairbanks with a pocketful of nothin'?

I realized Billy must still be pretty hungry. Those cookies probably only got his motor running. "I got a couple of bucks. You want a hamburger or something?"

Billy's eyes lit up. "Would I ever!"

"Well, let's go. I'm buyin'!"

"No, thanks. I'm cool. I'll be right here."

I let things be the way he wanted. It was all good. "Be right back," I said. I was halfway to the door when I turned and asked, "Will you think about going home?"

Billy smiled. I wanted to keep him that way, smiling at me across the open space with a moment of peace on his face.

I left in a hurry. There was loud traffic and horns blared at me as I zigzagged through the five o'clock rush of people heading home to their regular families. Dads in big cars going home to see their kids and sit at the dinner table with the whole family. I waved at people on the sidewalk and laughed when they stared at me, their faces covered with questions. I was glad they noticed me.

At the Big G, I spent my two dollars on their three-burgers-for-a-buck deal and then found an extra quarter in my pocket for a pop. Billy was waiting at the door when I returned, suddenly anxious.

"Here ya go. Chow down!" I said tossing the bag of burgers at him. Then I saw his face. "What's wrong, Billy? What is it?"

"I have to go." He stood back against the wall and rubbed his hands up and down his arms.

"What do you mean? Right now?"

"I have to go live with my mom in Oregon. We were just getting to be friends and now I have to go." Billy looked so sad again, like when he was talking about his dad dying.

"Yeah. Eat your damn burger," I said roughly as I commandeered one of the burgers for myself. "We can't do anything about anything, Billy. And you know it. At least you still got a mom."

"Good burger," he said with his mouth full.

"Haven't eaten much, huh?"

"Nope. Believe it or not, candy bars get kinda old and I've read every one of those comics a hundred times."

"You could have called. I wouldn't tell anybody."

"I know. Guess I'm an idiot."

"Takes one to know one." We laughed finally.

It took awhile after we ate to start the conversation again, so finally I stood up and said, "Come on. It's time to go."

I could tell when he was ready, so we walked out into the sun, and hopped on our bikes. As we rode away, I looked back at the Caribou Club and realized that when Billy told his story—and the police would want it all—the secret of our hangout would come out and maybe even be front-page news. I just kept reminding myself that a friend like Billy was worth it.

I was going to leave him at his driveway to make up with his grandma in his own time. When I turned to leave, he grabbed my arm.

"Hey, I was in the railroad yard, okay? I was hiding there and you found me 'cause I got scared and flagged you down." He talked fast outlining our lie, and it had to be a big one.

"You mean? Are you sure?" I said, nervous about telling yet another lie.

"Yeah, nothing about the club. I got it covered."

"You're the best liar I ever met," I said as he walked his bike into the carport.

He turned and smiled. "Takes one to know one."

It was two days before Billy was allowed to call me and by then cops had quizzed me about finding him. This time there was no trip to the police station, just a phone call and then a drop-by to "clarify some details." I held pretty tight to my story and played up how excited I was to find Billy okay.

When Billy called he said we needed to apologize to Mr. Martin and he didn't feel like calling the other guys even though they had a lot more to answer for. We met later that day at Mr. Martin's driveway and I was feeling pretty meek and squeamish about the whole thing. He had been really nice to us and probably had us figured for class A jerks.

When he answered the door, Mr. Martin looked us over and glared at us so I got hot and anxious. After an eternity he said, "Well, look what we got here. I heard they rounded you up, Billy.

Hope your ol' grandma beat your ass for that stunt. What were you thinkin', boy?"

Billy was all shaky and upset, but he stuck his chin out and met Mr. Martin's eyes. "I'm real sorry, Mr. Martin. I had no idea this would make trouble for you. You been good to me and you had none of this comin'."

"Yeah, I'm sorry too," I added, trying not to look away or down when I did it.

Mr. Martin leaned on his doorjamb, a grin slowly sneaking across his face. "Shoot, don't worry about me, boys. I been danced around by the cops before and probably will be again." Relief flooded through me and I could see Billy relax.

Mr. Martin continued, "But your granny, that's a different story. You did a hard one on her, boy, and she'll be awhile getting over it."

"Yeah, I know, sir. I really messed up and now they're sending me to Oregon. I guess this is good-bye."

He stuck out his hand to Mr. Martin, who took it and gave it a good shake. "All right, Billy, you keep your head screwed on, okay?"

"And you," he looked at me, "the cops said you stood up for me. Thank you."

"Yessir," I said, "but I'm sorry anyway."

"Okay then. I guess we're square." He held out his hand to me and I shook it like a man. Billy and I were across the street heading home when he hollered, "Hey, Sam. You wanna shovel snow this winter, earn a few bucks, you come on by. I'm getting old and lazy."

"Sure thing, Mr. Martin. Sounds good."

We hopped on our bikes and rode to the Big G and ate sundaes together. We didn't talk much. There wasn't much left to say.

Billy left for Oregon a couple days later, and that time in the Caribou Club eating three-for-a-buck burgers was our last time together. I figured he'd make new friends in Oregon since he was the kind of guy anybody would want for a pal. I hoped someday he would get a nice Corvette Stingray to drive through life.

On the way home, I tried to see ahead to the days between now and school. I was alone again, just like back in May. A homestead kid without friends in the big city.

Chapter 16

That Sunday after Billy left, Mom, Mary, and I took a trip to the Matanuska Valley for fresh vegetables like we used to grow ourselves. I think Mom did it to break me out of my funk about Billy leaving and summer ending. School was just a few weeks off and I was nervous about facing that first day alone.

For the first time in months, I could see more trees and rivers and mountains than houses or buildings, and I wanted to stay there. We drove past tractors baling hay and there were kids riding horseback across the freshly mown fields. Most places had acre after acre of potatoes.

"How would you like to hoe that field of potatoes, Sam?" Mom asked.

"No thanks!" I rubbed my hands on my pants leg, remembering my sore palms from last year's hoeing.

"Do you miss it?" she asked.

"Yeah, a little."

"You were getting to be quite the farmer last year, you know, when you used to help me in the garden."

"Seems like a long time ago, Mom."

The farmers were tending long rows of potatoes, carrots, and cabbage. We bought some lettuce and radishes from the stands that stood at the corner of the fields where a farm road met the highway. Mom cooed over each bit of produce, critiquing the varieties. Then she got weepy and walked back to the car.

She was smiling again when we found a place that offered you-pick raspberries. "Oh, kids, let's pick some and make jam. Wouldn't that just taste the best?"

Mary rolled her eyes. "Oh, Mother."

"Mary, you love strawberry jam. Sammy, you want to, don't you?"

My mind said, Not really, but I said, "Sure."

The farmer gave us little metal pails and pointed out where to pick. He chewed on a toothpick and talked raspberries with Mom. "Yeah, it was a good year for the berries, plenty of rain and a enough sun to keep things warm. You should find some good fat berries there."

Picking was slow at first, but within a few minutes, Mary and I had forgotten our resistance and picked along together, chatting with Mom in the August sun as if everything was just fine.

"How come you don't hang around with those dorky friends of yours anymore?" Mary asked, flipping a raspberry at my face.

"How do you know I don't?"

"'Cause they call when you're not home." She stopped picking and put a womanly hand on her hip. "You could always call my friend Janice you know." She giggled.

I slipped a handful berries in my mouth and said, "High

school girls don't hang out with dumb guys on stupid bicycles, you know."

"So what about your buddies?"

"I don't know. Like you said, they're dorks." I hurried on down the row in search of better picking. The field was feeling mighty small.

Then Mary surprised me. "You been hanging around down at that club, haven't you? Is that where you found Billy?"

"Maybe," I answered quietly.

"Maybe? Come on, Sam. Tell me. I heard there's gonna be a party there this Friday."

I froze. Even though I knew it would happen eventually, hearing it made it worse. "What?" I said. I didn't want to act too surprised, but I was.

"Yeah, I guess somebody found out about your little secret and now it's the place to be."

"So?"

"So, what do you think Mom would say about it? What's the word? Breaking and entering?"

A month ago, before Billy disappeared, I would have taken the bait and gone at it with Mary. Not anymore. "I don't think you're really gonna tell Mom. If she hears anything weird she'll have us both grounded and there will be no party for you either."

Mary's mouth was still open when I walked off down the row and set a full pail of berries on a table and walked out to lean on the car.

Across the road were a couple girls about my age cutting zucchinis and packing them in boxes. Each worked along a row, stooping to cut the green squash then lay them carefully in the cardboard boxes. At the end of the row they stood and stretched and shaded their eyes with dirty hands to look around. They peered at me eyeing them and waved. They had brown arms and ponytails bouncing above their tight sweaty T-shirts and cutoff jeans.

I was feeling alive and pretty bold, so I sauntered across the road. "Hi there. Looks like hot work."

One smiled at me. "You bet. Wanna help?"

"Yeah," said the other. "Don't just stand there gawking."

I hung there for a moment admiring their invitation, measuring the honesty of two pretty girls in the sun picking vegetables. But there was no chance to run and join them though my mind and body said, Yes, Yes, Yes!

"Sammy, Mom says it's time to go," Mary called with a laugh. "Say good-bye to your friends."

I waved halfheartedly to the farm girls, and trudged back to the car, glaring at Mary and wishing Billy had been there to help me flirt with those girls.

Mom was caught in the moment. "Look," she said, pointing to aspens lining the field. "Those leaves will be like gold coins when they turn. Another six weeks and they'll all be dead."

I didn't like her saying that word. Dead, death, dying. After I had worked for four months not to say it in front of her, like it was a new four-letter word, she said it herself and never flinched.

"We'll have to come back in the fall and see the leaves. Your father always liked the fall."

All the way home I tried to figure out what might be going through her mind. How did she feel about Dad now that he was gone? Did she ever wake up and forget he was dead? Did she still cry after we'd gone to bed?

On the one hand I wanted her to talk about Dad, to remember things, but on the other I could never bring him up around her.

That afternoon was the first time I'd heard her volunteer any comments about Dad in months.

Finally, Mom cleared her throat and said, "You know, kids, your dad's been gone most of a year now. I think maybe we're about out of the woods."

I leaned into her words, wanting more, waiting for stories to hang on to. But only silence followed, and we all wrapped ourselves in memories as we returned to the city.

Chapter 17

The next day I wasted no time getting to the club. I rode my bike through the weeds right to the back door. I wanted so badly for Mary to be wrong, but I knew she wasn't. If someone was planning a party, that meant they must have broken my lock to get in. Sure enough, my padlock hung open on the hasp, and the door wasn't even latched. I almost left right there and then, but unfamiliar courage pushed me inside the building.

It smelled mustier than I remembered and I couldn't see a thing. Someone had been there, all right, but the place was empty now. Empty of people, but not their garbage. When I flipped on the lights, I found the floor littered with smashed lightbulbs—tiny shards of glass were everywhere—and I knew that Taylor and Macek had been back playing at lightbulb grenades again. They must have broken every bulb in the place except the spotlights for the bandstand. When I found beer bottles and crushed cigarette butts as well, I knew that Mary had been right. Taylor and Macek had sold me out and given up the club to some older kids. She hadn't made any of it up, and I knew then that I had lost it all.

I spent an hour sweeping up broken glass and trash before I gave up and headed home. Just for spite I hung the lock back on the way I had it and hammered the nail flush with a rock so that getting in wouldn't be easy. They would know Sam Barger had been there. Taylor and Macek would know I was in on their betrayal.

I wanted a little joy in my life so I stopped at the Big G and sat at the counter staring at nothing. "Be right there," Shirley called from the far end of the counter. Then she turned back to giggle and slap a boy playfully on the shoulder. It wasn't Allen, but some new guy in a jean jacket. He was thick and blocky, but not tall, with straw-colored hair that he slicked back.

Eventually, Shirley made her way over to me with a glass of water. "Hey, you look like you lost your best friend."

"I guess I did," I said. Before I could say more she was fetching me a root beer.

"This will cheer you up," she said, "you'll see." And then she was back down to the end of the counter leaning over to chat with that guy again.

I barely tasted the root beer and was glad I didn't order a sundae because I wanted to be gone from there. I wanted to be gone from everywhere.

I spent the rest of the week just waiting for Friday. I couldn't forgive the hurt of losing the club to a bunch of older kids, but couldn't resist it either. I had to see how it looked full of people and music. When Friday night finally rolled around, I waited until eight o'clock, then told Mom I was running to the store for a minute, and took off.

By the time I got there, I could see teenagers already slipping through the brush and the club's back door. They had parked their cars at the ball field and worn a path around and through the alders. I counted at least three couples and a small group of guys who had gone in when music began to leak through the broken windows to where I hid in the alders. I could hear voices but I didn't recognize them and for some reason that mattered. I crept closer.

A few feet from the door, I recognized the song, and imagined the dance floor full of teenagers swaying in the dim light spilling off the bandstand. The music played, louder now through the open door, "You've Lost That Lovin' Feelin'" by the Righteous Brothers.

The music stopped and suddenly I stood pressed against the back of the building, just steps away from the door. I heard everything, my breath and thundering pulse, the traffic on C Street. Then for a moment there were no cars gunning up the hill and I could hear voices again from inside.

"See, I told you it was cool."

It was Macek! Dirty, stinkin', rotten Macek! His cocky voice bounced off the wall like a missed shot and I caught it hard. I was moving without thinking, in through the open door, down the hall, and into the main room. A circle of shadows hovered in the center of the dance floor, *my* dance floor. They were standing close together so I couldn't make out Macek or Taylor among them. The shapes were larger than I was used to. High schoolers. I could see four or five of them, and then suddenly I could see Macek, small and shadowed in their center.

"Macek, you bastard!" I used the word for the first time, and I tasted its power. Then immediately, the mass of bodies opened like a mouth and spit forth Macek.

"Sam! Hey, man, good to see you."

Wham! I hit him full force in the guts and followed him to the floor, pounding his body, arms, and head with my balled fists.

"You dirty bastard!" The power of the word was hot and strong and good.

Then hands had me and dragged me up and away from Macek, pinning my arms so I couldn't swing. That's when I saw Taylor back in the shadows, hiding a bit. And he was laughing. I thrashed against the strong arms holding me and kicked out at Taylor and got a slap on the face for it from some guy I didn't know.

"Get out!" I screamed. "You don't belong here! Go find your own place!" That got me slapped again, this time by a guy I did know. It was the guy from the diner. The one I saw flirting with Shirley. Here with the rest of the kids, he looked more like a man than a teenager.

"We like this place, shithead, so *you* get out," said the blond guy in the denim jacket. I could see the strength in him, and knew I wasn't going anywhere until he said I could.

"This is our party and I don't remember sending you an invitation," he said.

Behind the curtain the music started again and I saw three couples up on the bandstand moving out to dance in the light.

"This ain't your place anymore, kiddo."

I looked around at the kids Macek and Taylor had sold our secret to. They were all pretty big—bigger and older than me. I was alone and outnumbered, and I knew that the battle was lost before it really began.

Even if I beat Taylor and Macek and magically drove the others away, the secret was out. As lost as a thrown water balloon. It would tumble through space and shatter into a mass of water and rubber shreds that could only shrivel and disappear.

"What's going on?" called another voice I knew. It was coming from the darkness by the doorway. "You guys throw a party and not invite me?" The voice moved toward us, but stopped outside the circle of light. It was Allen. Mr. Perfect. I was able to spin around in the sweaty arm that held me so I could see him.

Allen squinted into the lights. "We under attack or something?"

The husky wrestler type who held my arms laughed. "Kinda."

The guy from the diner laughed also. "This kid busted in, uninvited, and punched our little buddy here. Foul-mouthed little creep, too."

"I can't believe you hang out with these jerks!" I said to Allen, trying to sound tough.

That got me slapped a third time. "I didn't say you could talk, you little puke," growled Mr. Denim Jacket. There was more threat in his voice this time, and he leaned in so close I could smell the cigarette smoke in his clothes.

"Wait a minute. . . . Is that you, Sam?" Allen asked, friendly as can be. He turned hard eyes on my captors. "Tell your buddy to let him go, Stark. Sam's a friend of mine."

"But this little moron's askin' for it."

"So are you!"

I could feel the tension in the room rise as the hold on my arms relaxed, and I pulled loose. Then I knew I was right about Stark. He was the guy in the denim jacket from the Big G. He was the guy I'd seen with Shirley. Until that moment I never thought much of it, but obviously Allen had.

Allen stepped back from the group. He hooked his thumbs in his front pockets and did a James Dean pose. "What are you guys doing here?" Allen asked, like this was his private home and we were intruders.

"It's mine. Ask those little rats over there," I said, pointing to Macek and Taylor.

"What's yours? This place?" asked Stark. Everybody laughed except Allen. And Macek. He had retreated to stand next to Taylor and nurse his pride. "Lot of people seem mixed up about what's theirs tonight." Stark stared over at Allen, a strange look on his face. It felt like they were continuing a conversation they had started earlier.

Then, in the background by the bandstand curtains, I saw Shirley step out into the light. She stood with her arms folded across her blouse, her hair perfect and wavy. Allen saw her too, and he looked back and forth between her and Stark. Suddenly, Stark and Allen seemed to be in the center of the room with the rest of us in the shadows around them.

Stark's group moved toward Allen and the room felt small and hot. I realized that Allen and I might be on the same side or at least in the same boat: mad and outnumbered. "I found this place first," I said, "*me*. Me and Billy Anderson."

Billy's name fell like a cast spell, lengthening the shadows and bringing the mass of bodies back together in the center of the light.

"You mean the kid that got wasted?" Stark asked.

Wasted? They still thought he was missing or dead. Guess the word hadn't gotten out yet that he'd been found and now was gone again. Billy was so totally gone, in fact, that it seemed stupid that he had so much power over these kids.

"Yeah," I said, "does that scare you?"

"Oh yeah, kid, I'm wetting my pants I'm so scared," laughed Stark. He slapped the blond kid next to him on the back, a smiling face ravaged by pimples.

"Oh my," said Pimple Face, "do I hear a ghost? OOOWAA!"

"You're not funny!" I yelled again, my frustration building. "You're just a bunch of jerks. Get out of here!"

Pimple Face kicked at me with a pointed black boot that I knocked away. "Come on!" I challenged, foolish and desperate, "I'm not afraid of you, zit face!"

Allen grabbed me then and dragged me away. "Easy, big fella." He walked me off away from the crowd, all the time looking back at Shirley. "How'd you find this place?" he asked, trying to calm me down I guess. "I always thought it was just an old building with nothing inside."

When I didn't answer, he kept going. "Anyway, you need to get out of here. You don't want to mess with these guys."

I was too busy trying not to cry to answer. That's what I wanted: to cry with no one around to gawk. I was supposed to be too old for that, but it was cry or hit somebody. Allen patted me on the back and looked around at the soda fountain, counter, and lines of stools. I could tell he was getting carried away in his imagination.

"This could be such a cool club. We could have dances with bands and food."

"You want me to get out and leave it for you and your buddies, right?"

"What?" He had stopped listening to me and turned to look at Shirley and Stark standing close in the shadows.

"Just like always—high schoolers only. We'd be left out." I walked away.

"They're not my buddies," I heard him say. Mr. Perfect didn't understand. Nice as he was, Allen was just like everyone else who seemed to lose their memory as soon as they turned sixteen and forgot all about what it was like to be young and out of place, a kid nobody wants around.

I was heading for the door when three more guys walked in. "Wow, holy crap," said the first one in. "There's a ton of cars out there. I think everybody on this side of town is crashing your party, Stark." I pushed past them into the doorway and was met by a rush of bodies. A cluster of jeans and T-shirts came through, pushing me back inside.

That's when I saw the fight.

I couldn't hear the words between them, but I didn't need to. I watched Allen, tall and graceful, dance in toward Stark. He squared his stance and punched Stark in the side of the head. Stark was caught off guard and staggered back, then came at Allen like a heavyweight boxer. He crouched low, ready to pound Allen with both fists. For a moment, Allen was Muhammad Ali, bobbing and weaving to avoid Stark's long-arm jabs.

Then the ring of kids closed in with Stark's buddies cheering him on while I stood frozen at the edge of the dance floor. The circle around the fighters was tight and someone pushed Allen in the back, making him stumble forward. Stark grappled with Allen until he was able to wrestle him to the floor and punch him hard on the back of the head. Allen rolled free, but when he stood up, the big guy was waiting and pounded his fist into Allen's torso, his chest, his head—until Allen went down.

Stark was stomping around Allen and yelling so I could hear him now, "I oughta kick your guts in!" Allen was still and looked like he was maybe passed out. I could see blood leaking out of his nose and mouth. One eye was closed and already starting to swell.

"Give it to him!" someone shouted, and Stark moved in to kick with his heavy work boots. Allen caught his foot and pulled Stark down so he landed hard on his back. Allen rolled away and stood up. Suddenly, it was Allen on his feet and Stark trying to get up.

Behind the fight, Shirley was standing at the curtain biting her lip. The music was back on and the Rolling Stones sang the words to their song "Satisfaction."

Then Shirley screamed. Stark was getting to his feet and I could see something shining in his hand. It was a knife. A switchblade. He pressed a button on the handle and the blade flashed out. The force of its presence seemed to fill the room. Someone gasped—I think it was Shirley. I hoped it was.

"Allen!" I screamed.

I wanted him to run, to back away from blade, but he was past that and went toward Stark instead, challenging him.

"Come on! Come on, you coward!" he yelled.

And then I was running. Not away, where I wanted to run, but toward them, toward the fight. Pimple Face stepped in my path, trying to block me, but I ran right through him, knocking him to the floor.

Stark and Allen lunged at each other without touching. I leaped past them and up onto the bandstand. Out of the corner of my eye I could see Stark lunge again. Allen stumbled backward and slipped, almost falling.

I reached behind the curtains and hit the light switch. The room went pitch black. I could hear Allen and Stark shuffling and grunting below me. Then the place was suddenly silent except for the heavy breathing of the two fighters.

"Cops! Cops out front!" someone near the door yelled. There was a mad scramble for the back door.

I jumped off the bandstand and toward the fighters. I found Allen and grabbed his arm. "This way," I whispered. "Don't follow them."

My eyes were adjusting to bits of light coming in through

the boarded-up windows, so it was easy to find the broken window we had escaped through so long ago. I kicked out the plywood and climbed out. I reached in and grabbed Allen under the armpit to help him through. He flinched. "Don't touch me," he groaned. "Hurts too much." He climbed out on his own, but too slowly. I was worried the cops would walk back around.

Allen's Chevy was parked in front of the club, so I didn't have to look for it. There was a cop car parked next to it, but it was empty. I could hear the cop yelling around back. Allen staggered to the passenger side and tossed the keys to me.

"You gotta drive," he moaned. "I can't do it." He had his hand pressed over his ribs, and when he lifted it up I could see blood soaking his white T-shirt in an ever-widening circle. And there was a darker gash across his ribs. Stark had gotten him with that knife.

Before I could protest, Allen was inside the car. I slid into the driver's seat and under the car's dome light I got a better look at how messed up Allen was: one eye was swollen shut and the other had a big cut above it with blood running down one cheek. I could see blood oozing from beneath his hands, where they were pressed to his ribs. It was already dripping down his arm and onto the car seat.

He moaned and leaned his head back. I thought he was fainting. Then he mumbled something and his head flopped down onto his chest.

"What'd you say, Allen?"

He raised his eyes to mine and spoke more clearly. "Don't tell me you can't drive a stick shift."

"Well, uh . . ." I started to protest. Then I shook my head. "I can do it."

I was shaking so much I dropped the car keys and it took forever to find them and get the right one in the ignition. I looked at the patrol car and knew the cop could help us and call an ambulance, but that meant more trouble. So I jammed the car in gear and hit the gas. I silently gave thanks that Dad and Joe had let me drive the jeep up and down the beach last summer.

The clutch and gas pedals didn't feel the same as the jeep, and we stalled a couple times before we got out of that parking lot. On reflex, I drove down Hollywood Drive a couple of blocks and then pulled into an alley and parked. I was panting like I'd run a mile, and I really wanted to drive and drive until we were far away from the Caribou Club. But Allen was bleeding and I had to know where and how bad.

With a bit of gasping and groaning from Allen I got a look at the wounds. The knife had slashed across his ribs and gashed his arm. The rib wound was deep, but I couldn't tell how deep. The arm was bleeding the most. Allen kept mumbling and pushing my hands away, but I managed to wrap his arm in a towel I found in the backseat. I slipped out of my jacket and pulled my T-shirt off, which I wadded up and pressed against the rib slash. Allen gritted his teeth but other than that he was silent, staring out into the night.

"Hold this," I told him, placing his left hand on the makeshift bandage. "You're going to be okay. The cuts aren't bad." I wasn't sure I believed what I was telling him, but I needed to tell him something.

As scared as I was for Allen, I couldn't help but notice the blood staining the white leather seats of his pride and joy.

"It's my hand that hurts the most," he said after I'd bandaged his cuts.

"You mighta broken it when you hit Stark in the head."

"Pretty stupid, huh? Over a girl."

"He had it coming. What a jerk!"

Allen chuckled weakly. "He had it coming, but I'm the one who got it." He went slack again, and I thought he fainted.

I turned back to the wheel and fumbled to find first gear. "Don't worry, I'll get you to the hospital." I found the gear and pulled out of the alley.

"No," Allen snapped.

"Oh man, you need a doctor. You're a mess."

"No doctor," he insisted. "Just take me home, Sam. Dad'll know what to do. Take me home. It's just down the street." He was sounding weak again. "Really, really close."

I didn't know what to do. I didn't know what the right choice was. But I did know that if I still had a dad, that's what I'd want, too. To be with him.

"Okay, Allen, let's get you home," I said, easing out onto the street.

Allen laid his head back again. "Thanks, Sam. You're a life-saver. I should never have hit Stark in the head. I should never have hit him at all."

I didn't say a word because I had just then realized that I was driving a '57 Chevy two-door hardtop down Hollywood Drive with a beat-up varsity letterman bleeding all over the front seat.

Chapter | 8

I got to Allen's house and had a few tense minutes at the front door when I had to explain to his dad why I was bringing his son home all cut up. In the end, his dad looked me in eye and said calmly, "You did right thing."

Mr. Hanson asked if I was okay, then helped his son out of the car. I took that opportunity to head home, but he called me back. "Young man," he said in a calm and steady voice, "I hope we can count on you to keep this between us. Nobody else's business."

"Yessir," I agreed. "You can count on me."

Allen reached out his good hand and when I took it he said, "You didn't lose that club, Sam. You just found it for everybody else. It'll work out. You'll see."

We shook hands and that was that.

The TV news was on when I got home and I heard a reporter talking about police responding to a teen party on Government Hill. I acted indifferent when Mom said, "Thank goodness you're home safe and sound. I hope your sister is behaving herself."

"I'm sure she is, Mom," I answered. "I'm sure she is."

I was asleep almost as soon as my head hit the pillow. When I awoke in the middle of the night I could hear it was raining. I went to the bathroom to pee, but when I got there something grabbed my gut and thrust it up into my throat. I could see Stark leering with that switchblade in his hand and Shirley biting her lip. I could see Allen's blood on the car seat, smell it on my hands. I vomited, kneeling and hugging the toilet as tears dripped into my mouth.

I crept back to bed, curled up under my quilt, and listened to the rain. Morning was a long way off and that was good for the rain and me and the quilt. When day came, the brightness gave me hope.

Mom was sleeping on the couch under an afghan when I sneaked out to buy a morning paper. The *Sunday Daily News* was a big wad under my arm as I trotted up the sidewalk and the stairs to our door. I had been temped to open it right at the stand, but I waited. In my room I could read it, as if the ritual of reading and seeing the whole story would ease my guilt, fear, or anger.

I spread the front page out on my quilt. There was the Caribou Club. The story told of a teen gang fight broken up by the quick response of the police department. I read every word, even following the stories that had more questions than answers. No charges filed. No injuries reported. There was a profile on the building itself, one official calling it a "public nuisance." I concluded that the cops knew about the fight but not who was involved. There was a chance that Allen and I would never be identified and that was fine with me.

That day, I went for a bike ride along the bluff where I had first met Billy. I couldn't sit around home waiting for the police to come *again* and take me downtown *again*, and ask me questions *again*. So I roamed the bluff trails and tried to forget.

All around me little kids were riding bikes over the trails in the sunshine. They laughed and challenged each other to try new and bigger bumps. Through the alders I could hear other kids playing on the swings and teeter-totter. One high-pitched voice was chanting, "Teeter-totter, bread and water, wash your face in dirty water." I zigzagged through the brush until I could see Melissa. She rose suddenly from behind the green fringe then dropped out of sight and a tiny black head rose opposite her, then she rose again, lifting her hands toward the clouds and making me smile.

I passed beyond the playground, through a barren lot I had visited the first days at the apartment. Its sides were too steep for bikes, so there were no trails through it, just fireweed and alders. Leaving my bike, I made my own trail into the green out of the brown and gray. Except for the pop cans and beer bottles, I could have been sitting on the bluff above our beach sites on Cook Inlet.

The brush rustled before me and a pair of brown wings thrashed the air. I leaped aside, then laughed out loud at the grouse, which ended his flight on the branch of a cottonwood sapling only yards away.

"I could hit you with a rock from here," I warned. The grouse clucked and bobbed its head.

Beneath that tree, I made a nest for my thoughts and dreamed up a tale of building the railroads through Alaska. I made great roads with beds of gravel and paved with steel. I cut spruce and birch trees, laying their trunks across the bogs so I could cross the muskeg. When the first engines coughed their way into view, dragging a string of squealing, clanking cars, I crossed the mountains and lived with the Indians. The dreams were getting strong again, and I found I could go for an hour without thinking of anything real.

But I couldn't get away for long. Mostly, I couldn't get away from Allen and Shirley, Allen and Stark, Shirley and Stark. I was starting to see how complicated life could be. I had made Allen into Mr. Perfect and admired the way he had it all together. He was the cool older guy that kids like me envied. Now he was probably feeling as much a loser as me. Who would ever imagine Mr. Perfect getting dumped by a girl? Losing a fight? Being rescued by a fourteen-year-old secondhand friend.

I waited several days to hear from the police or from Allen, but I heard nothing and was haunted by the silence. I could only think that Allen and his dad decided not to press charges and nobody else gave names to the police. I was restless and lost, living in limbo.

Finally, I gathered the courage to ride my bike to the Caribou Club. I intended to just cruise by, but when I saw work trucks in the parking lot, I turned in and bounced through the potholes. Instead of sneaking around back, I rode straight to the front door and found it standing open. There were paint buckets and drop cloths and a radio was playing country music. On the side of the building I found a man on a ladder. Fresh paint covered nearly half of the building already, making it seem taller.

"Hey, kid, looking for a job?"

"No. Just looking."

The man on the ladder was small and round with a face like Santa Claus. "Looks pretty good, don't it?" he said. He had stopped painting and leaned back to admire his work. I agreed with him and dared to ask another question.

"Why are you painting it?"

"'Cause they're paying me to." He laughed at his own joke and I smiled. "The city bought the place, I guess."

Idly I tested the paint and my finger came away with a spot of cream. To my right was our broken window, the escape hatch we used when the cop locked us in. I remembered the dry tight choking I felt that day. "What are they going to do with it?"

"Turning it into a teen center. Can you believe it? One more place for you kids to come and spend your parents' money and get in trouble." He pointed to a sign leaned up against the building. The looping modern-style letters read: "The Hangout."

The man climbed down from his ladder. "Big gang rumble here the other night, I hear. Big fight."

"Oh yeah?"

"Cop came by here the other day. Said it was just two boys fightin' over a girl, then a couple buddies jumped in and the kid was outnumbered. One of those eastside-westside things, like in the movies. One pulled a knife and the other lost."

He took off his hat and scratched the remains of his hair. "Lucky somebody didn't get killed." He shook his head. "It don't make sense. Fightin' over a girl like that."

"Better fix that window," I said.

"Huh?"

I pointed at the window Taylor had kicked out back in July. "Somebody might break in."

I laughed at my own joke and left him muttering something about smart-aleck kids while he stirred more of the cream-colored paint. I walked my bike across the gravel one last time and turned up the wrong street when I reached the top. I had to ride past two blocks of strange houses to get back to Hollywood Drive and the Big G.

I had a quarter in my pocket, enough for a root beer. I ordered from a redheaded woman with a wedding ring and too much makeup. She smelled like old perfume and called me "sweetie."

As I pushed on the door open on my way out, my hand pressed a small poster announcing: "Teen Center Grand Opening! End of Summer Dance! All high school students welcome."

Chapter 19

The night of the big dance was the last Friday before school started, and I felt lost. All that day I moped around our apartment flopping on the couch, flipping through magazines. About once a week Mom took over the dinner cleanup job and did a top to bottom wipe down. She was halfway across the cupboards with a rag when I blurted out, "Mom, can we take a ride? I want to show you something."

"What's that?" she said, like she was expecting a picture I'd drawn or a cut on my knee.

"We have to go somewhere. In the car. Please."

Mom was already in her robe and she hated to go out after dinner. Her day was done. But for once she just got her coat and purse and went. It was as if I had used some powerful voice magic on her. No put-off, no questions. She just went. I know now she must have been paying more attention than I thought, she must have sensed my need.

"What is it you want to show me?" she asked as we motored through a drizzle on Hollywood Drive.

"Just wait, Mom. Just wait."

She was shooting skeptical glances my way, and I was glad the drive would only take five minutes, because her patience wouldn't last ten. As we approached the intersection by the Texaco station, I saw long lines of cars spraying water through the headlights as they turned left in front of us.

We parked on the hill above the club, the hill where I crashed on a bike a million days ago. Below us a stream of cars drained from the river of traffic and flowed into the gravel and puddles of the old Caribou Club.

Mom pulled a pack of cigarettes out of her purse and lit one. "What in the world are all those cars doing here? I thought this place was closed. More to the point, what are we doing here?"

"It *was* closed. The club I mean. That's what I wanted to show you."

"Why? What does this have to do with me?"

"Not you. Me. It has to do with me. I found it. The club. And I opened it, that's what. Me and Billy and the other guys." I leaned into the dashboard groping for support.

Mom looked at me. It was a shocked look, like I'd just admitted to murder. "What on earth are you talking about?"

"We opened it, Mom. Now listen. Just listen and don't kill me or anything. We found a way to get in. . . ."

The cigarette fell from her lips and she fumbled for it. "You . . . you broke in?"

"Yeah, kinda. But we didn't break anything. Just a window, but only because we had to get out when a cop locked us in." Her eyes widened. "Oh, that's not what I wanted to tell you." I was racing a train to the crossing. I had to talk fast before she got upset or quit listening, or both.

"We wanted a hangout, you know, like a fort. Our own place. Anyway, it's this really neat ballroom with lights and a bandstand and a restaurant part, and we cleaned it up. And the lights worked and, and—"

"And then you lost it? Is that what this is about? You lost something that wasn't yours in the first place?"

I started crying. "It *was* ours, Mom. Nobody was using it. And they just took it." I pulled a newspaper clipping out of my pocket, wiping my nose on a sleeve as I passed it over to my mom. I just wanted everything to be different. For her to know, for somebody to know, that I did it first. I started the whole thing.

"Don't wipe your nose on your sleeve." Mom handed me a tissue from her purse. It smelled of her and gum and leather. She read the newspaper out loud, leaning toward the dome light and letting the cigarette smoke curl up through the glow:

An abandoned nightclub gained new life this summer when a group of young people looking for a place to dance opened a side door and set about cleaning the old Caribou Club. A police investigation reported a break-in, but found that the youths had cleaned the rubbish and broken furniture from the lounge and ballroom. Rather than breaking windows and vandalizing, these energetic young people had the building in tiptop shape.

Unfortunately, on August 20th, violence erupted between rival gangs of thugs and several young people were reported hurt. Hoping to prevent further unsupervised gatherings by providing teens a safe meeting place, the city has leased the property and opened a teen club for the city's youth.

"You did this?" Her face was confused. "Do the police know you did this?"

"Yes, we did it. No, they don't know it was us."

"Who got hurt?"

"It was Allen, the kid who fixed my bike. But he's okay now. It was a fight over a girl. It wasn't gangs at all."

"Thank goodness."

With her blessing, I was off and running again. "See, we found it first, me and Billy. We cleaned it up. And believe me, it was a mess. We hung out there a few times, but then the high school kids with their hotshot cars found out and they took it away from us. That's where Allen got into it with Stark over Shirley. Just teenage stuff... he was fighting over a girl and pow!"

"I didn't know about any of this." Mom pulled her coat up around her shoulders and looked squarely into my face. "So since when does a son of mine break into a building, empty or not?"

"We weren't trying to steal anything. We were just hanging out."

"Wasn't it locked?"

"Well . . . sort of. There was this little door with a crummy lock and it just sorta jiggled open."

I had her undivided attention. I told her about how the club was dark and spooky and dirty when we first found it. I explained how the lights were left on and how neat the bandstand looked with the colored lamps shining on it. I told her almost everything. I told her about the fort and the Quonset hut and that Billy wasn't hiding in the railroad yard, but he was in the club. I told her I wasn't friends with Macek and Taylor anymore. But I didn't tell her the rest. She couldn't handle the story about Stark and Allen or about me driving him home. That would have been too much.

"You're sure you didn't break in?" I wasn't off the hook until she was sure, until she could find a way to justify all of this to herself.

"Yes, Mom! Don't you see? I wasn't breaking in because it was mine! It was mine and they took it. They took it just like they took the tree fort back home, just like they took Dad. And now everything is secondhand. My bike. This apartment. Don't you get it? We had everything just perfect at the club, it was brand-new, and now I'm stuck with nothing but a hand-me-down life that nobody else wants."

My mother's arms reached for my pain. "Oh, honey. Your dad is dead; nobody took him. And your tree fort, it's still there where you left it. We'll go back. It's still our house. But we have to make a new home here. I didn't want to come either, away from our friends and our home. But I had to. It's the only way."

"We had the fish sites. You let them go." All of the wrongs I had felt all summer came pouring out and I just cried. It was like all the sad I'd been saving up since Dad died suddenly flowed out of me. I sat and cried with Mom's hand on my back and her talking softly, like when I was little. And for the first time in a long while, being little felt good.

When I felt too weak to keep crying and the stinging stopped in my eyes, Mom and I sat and watched the parking lot fill up below us. The couples walked like Siamese twins straight through the open doors. Clutches of girls zigzagged through the cars with their heads together, giggling and pointing with their hairdos. Packs of boys in groups of three and four came in at angles and skulked about the edges of the lighted entrance. Cars raced their engines and then quieted when they passed the police cars watching from the shadows. We could see it all from our spot on the hill where I first crashed Billy's bike and first saw the Caribou Club. We listened to music I couldn't dance to.

Finally, Mom started the car and patted my leg. "You'll be going to dances sooner than you think, son," she said. And I knew then that she did understand, a little.

★ ✸

School started the following week, and I could feel the hint of frost in the air as I walked to the bus stop for the first time. Mary had pegged my pants for me so they fit tight all the way down the leg. We had reached a simple truce: I traded a day of house cleaning for her sewing. I used my basement cleaning money to buy a pair of pointed shoes like the Beatles wore. No more Sears and Roebuck's jeans and canvas sneakers for me. My sleeves I rolled up to the elbows.

At the bus stop, I stood with a blond kid in a leather jacket, and we waited coolly leaning on a light post, as if mourning the end of summer. We watched the grade school kids with new shoes and lunch boxes as they formed a noisy line, each wanting to be first on the bus. A cluster of pimple-faced high school boys stood smoking by a parked car, watching the girls in their new hairdos and short skirts. A black kid I'd seen around the apartments stopped to share our lamppost.

"You were Billy's friend," he said. "Cool guy. Too bad he split."

"Yeah, it's too bad. He was a good friend."

"Goin' back to school's a real drag," the blond kid said, scuffing the sidewalk with new Keds.

I smiled. "Yeah, but then summer was kind of a bummer, too."

Just then the bus arrived, and we followed the younger kids on without comment.

My first class was English and I sat next to a girl in a mini-skirt with a smile that reminded me of hamburgers. I smiled at her, and hoped she didn't have a boyfriend with a car.

"Hi, I'm Sandy," she said when she saw me looking at her. She had light brown hair to her shoulders that bounced when she talked.

Before I could answer, the bell rang, and a woman's voice at the front of the room cleared itself for nine months of talking.

"Welcome to freshman English. I am Mrs. Herzog. We are going to start right off with writing an essay. I have written the first line on the board for you. Now let's see what you can do with it."

Written on the board in perfect cursive were the words, "This summer was exciting because. . . ."

I smiled. Sandy smiled at me. Then I chuckled and blushed a little. Was I going to cry, right here in front of a girl named Sandy in a miniskirt and thirty other kids that I didn't know?

"Keep it quiet, young man." Mrs. Herzog was short and lean in a dark dress. She stood on her toes to peer down the row at me. "Save your jokes for the lunchroom, young man. Remember you want to start the school year on the right foot."

Sandy smiled again.

I wanted to tell Mrs. Herzog that neither of my feet felt right. I wanted to tell her that watching a girl undress was exciting or that a car wreck was exciting—but scary. I wanted to tell her that it was exciting when your dad is dead but you don't believe it, and when your friend isn't dead but you believed he was. I wanted to tell her that exciting really meant "scary as hell," like Stark or railroad cops.

But I didn't tell her any of that. She didn't deserve to know.

Instead of writing, I sat and stared at Sandy while she wrote long smooth sentences with large round letters, filling the pages of her notebook with endless strands of blue lace. I studied the curve of her thigh reaching out from her skirt and down past the knee to where the lightly tanned skin disappeared into her knee socks. I looked at the way her lips were pursed and serious, the bottom one disappearing into her mouth as she chewed it, writing without looking up.

I felt warm and unsafe as I wondered if Sandy knew how to dance. Then I wrote at the top of my paper: "This summer was exciting because I was famous and nobody knew it."

DISCUSSION QUESTIONS

1. Why does Sam take up trapping after his father dies?

2. How does his father's death change life for Sam's mom?

3. Why does Sam quit writing to Becky, his old girlfriend?

4. All through this story, Sam is involved with cars. Discuss the role of cars in the boys' lives.

5. Although they've just met, why does Sam find it easy to be friends with Billy?

6. How did girls influence Sam's development through the story?

7. Why is the fort the boys build in the gully unacceptable to Sam?

8. How does Sam's imagination work against him? For him?

9. How is life in Anchorage of 1965 different from today?

10. In what ways is Anchorage like a wilderness to Sam?

11. What is the basis for the close friendship between Sam and Billy?

12. What qualities make Macek and Taylor such poor choices as friends?

13. Why does the older boy, Allen, befriend Sam?

14. Why did Sam quit being friends with Macek and Taylor?

15. Why does Sam keep doing things that are scary and/or illegal?

16. Why does Sam seem to both admire and dislike Allen?

17. How does Sam's attitude change about lying?

18. Why is the Caribou Club so important to Sam?

19. When Sam finally tells his mom all about the Caribou Club, why does he say that his is a secondhand, hand-me-down life?

20. At the end of the book, Sam says that he was famous and nobody knew it. Why does he say this?

CPSIA information can be obtained at www.ICGtesting.com
Printed in the USA
BVOW06*1414240716

456681BV00019B/200/P

9 781943 328796